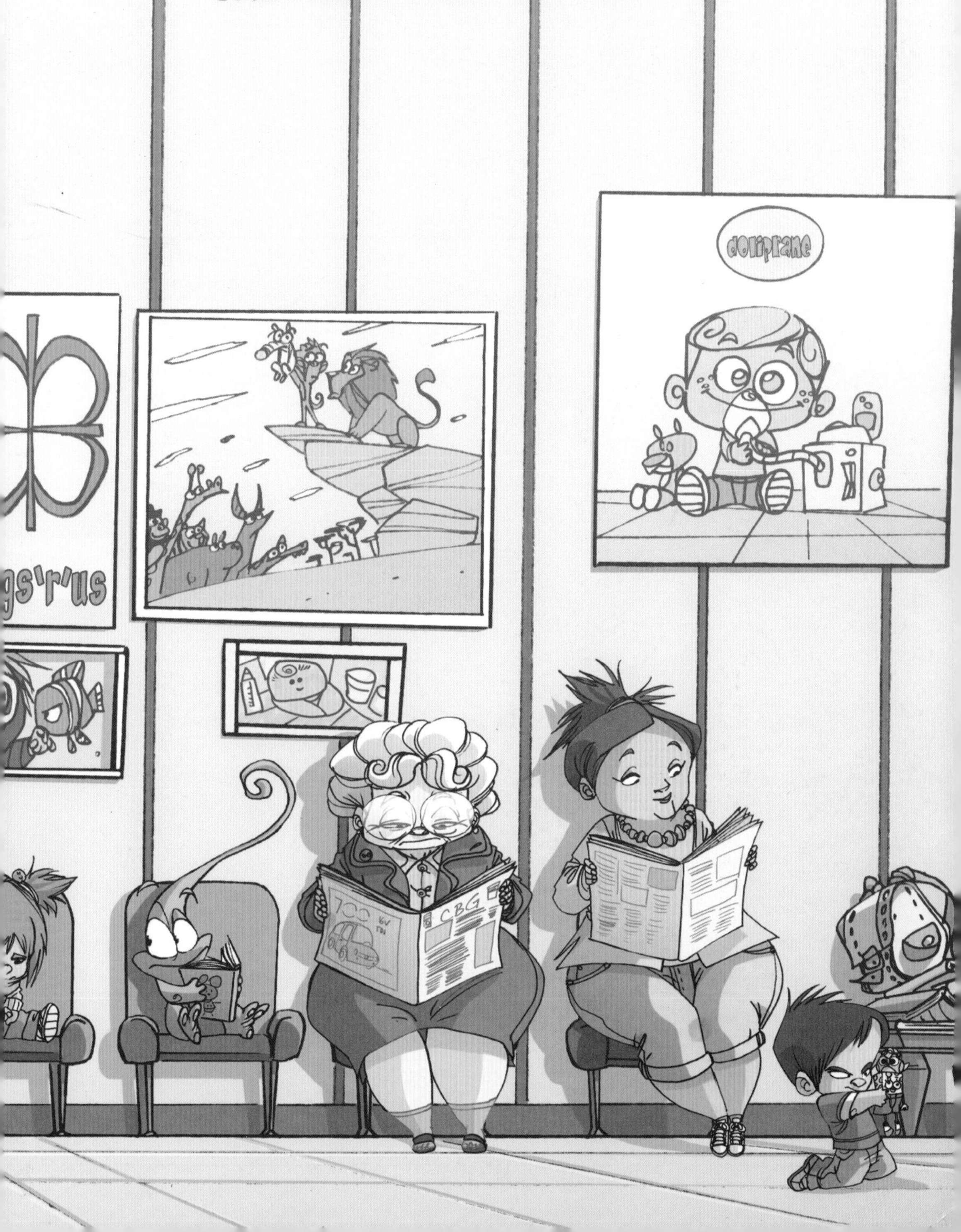
doliprane
gs'r'us
CBG

"The School of Nonsense"

Guillaume Bianco – Writer
Antonello Dalena – Artist
Cecilia Giumento – Colorist

PAPERCUTZ™
New York

This graphic novel is dedicated to Elisabetta and Susanna.
-Antonello

This graphic novel is dedicated to Zoé.
-Guillaume

Daddy

He's an artist. A painter... like Picasso, but better! We have lots of fun together when mommy's at work... He's the funniest daddy of all!

Mommy

She's the most beautiful mommy of all! She's not at home a lot because of her job, but she always finds time to cook my favorite food for me: "steak and fries with ketchup and mayonnaise!"

Coralie

She's my big sister. I adore her, even if, ever since she's been in her rebellious stage, she stays in her room all the time.

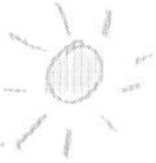

Ernest

He's a microbe... and he's my best friend! I caught him one day while on a frog hunt. Since then, we're always together... He's super smart and really strong: he can change into anything!

Sam

He's my mom's fiancé. He's nice, but I'm suspicious he's really some kind of evil germ trying to contaminate our family unit.

And me: Rebecca!

I'm not very big... It's 'cause I hate soup! I'd rather eat ketchup and chase frogs with Ernest in the rain!

Ernest & Rebecca graphic novels available from **PAPERCUTZ**™

Graphic Novel #1 "My Best Friend is a Germ"

Graphic Novel #2 "Sam the Repulsive"

Graphic Novel #3 "Grandpa Bug"

Graphic Novel #4 "The Land of Walking Stones"

Graphic Novel #5 "The School of Nonsense"

ERNEST & REBECCA graphic novels are available at booksellers everywhere. Or order online from papercutz.com. Or call 1-800-886-1223, Monday through Friday, 9-5 EST.© MC, Visa, and AmEx accepted. Available in hardcover only, #1 & #2 are $11.99 each, #3 and #4 on are $10.99 each. To order by mail, please add $4.00 for postage and handling for first book ordered, $1.00 for each additional book and make check payable to NBM Publishing. Send to: Papercutz, 160 Broadway, Suite 700, East Wing, New York, NY 10038.

Ernest & Rebecca
#5 "The School of Nonsense"

Guillaume Bianco – Writer
Antonello Dalena – Artist
Cecilia Giumento – Colorist
Jean-Luc Deglin – Original Design
Joe Johnson – Translation
Janice Chiang – Lettering
Beth Scorzato – Production Coordinator
Michael Petranek – Associate Editor
Jim Salicrup
Editor-in-Chief

© DALENA – BIANCO – ÉDITIONS DU LOMBARD
(DARGAUD-LOMBARD S.A.) 2013
www.lombard.com
All rights reserved.
English Translation and other editorial matter
Copyright © 2014 by Papercutz.
ISBN: 978-1-62991-045-1

Printed in China
September 2014 by New Era Printing LTD.
Unit C, 8/F, Worldwide Centre
123 Chung Tau Street, Hong Kong

Distributed by Macmillan
First Papercutz Printing

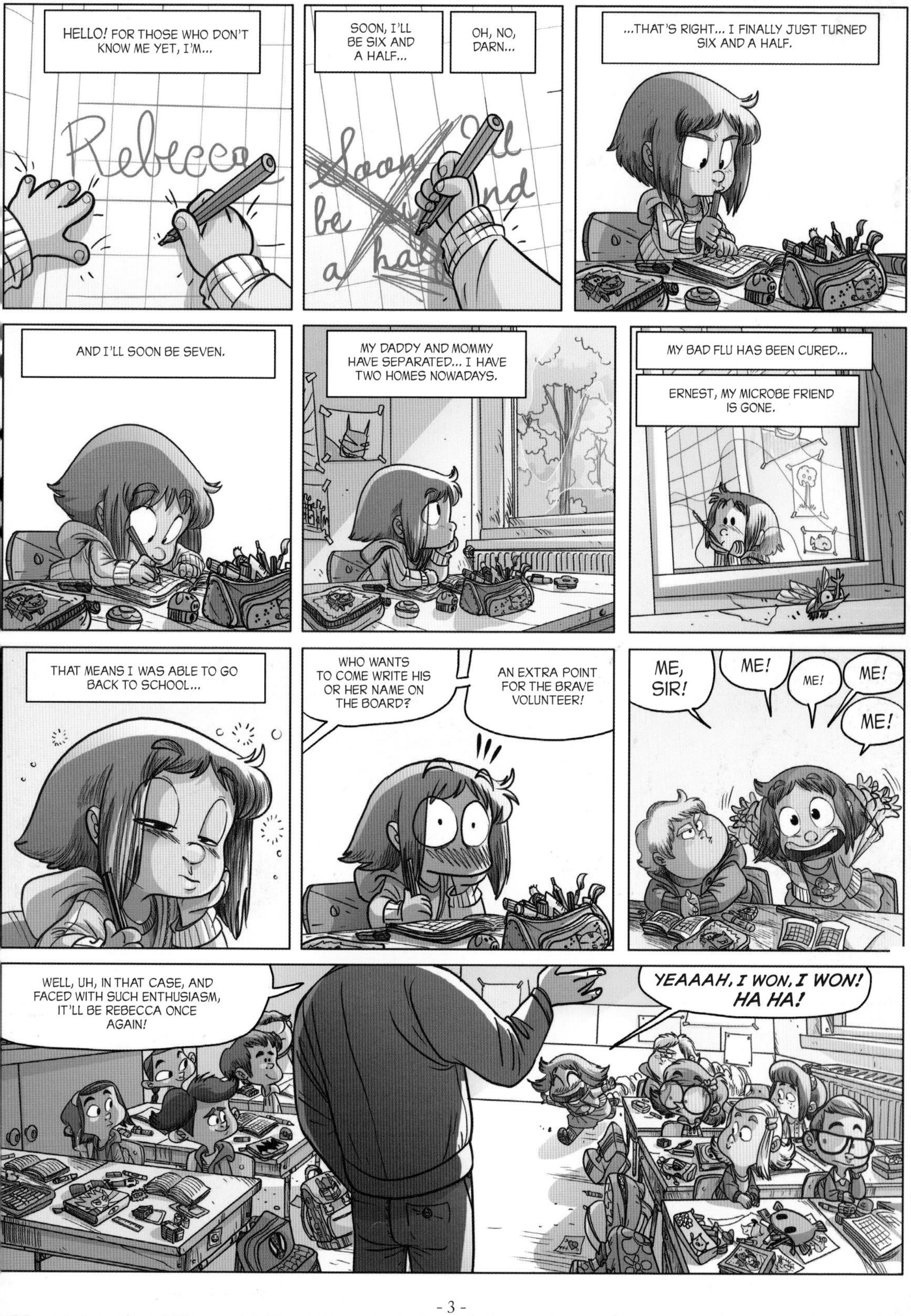

HELLO! FOR THOSE WHO DON'T KNOW ME YET, I'M...
Rebecca
SOON, I'LL BE SIX AND A HALF...
OH, NO, DARN...
...THAT'S RIGHT... I FINALLY JUST TURNED SIX AND A HALF.
AND I'LL SOON BE SEVEN.
MY DADDY AND MOMMY HAVE SEPARATED... I HAVE TWO HOMES NOWADAYS.
MY BAD FLU HAS BEEN CURED...
ERNEST, MY MICROBE FRIEND IS GONE.
THAT MEANS I WAS ABLE TO GO BACK TO SCHOOL...
WHO WANTS TO COME WRITE HIS OR HER NAME ON THE BOARD?
AN EXTRA POINT FOR THE BRAVE VOLUNTEER!
ME, SIR!
ME!
ME!
ME!
ME!
WELL, UH, IN THAT CASE, AND FACED WITH SUCH ENTHUSIASM, IT'LL BE REBECCA ONCE AGAIN!
YEAAAH, I WON, I WON! HA HA!

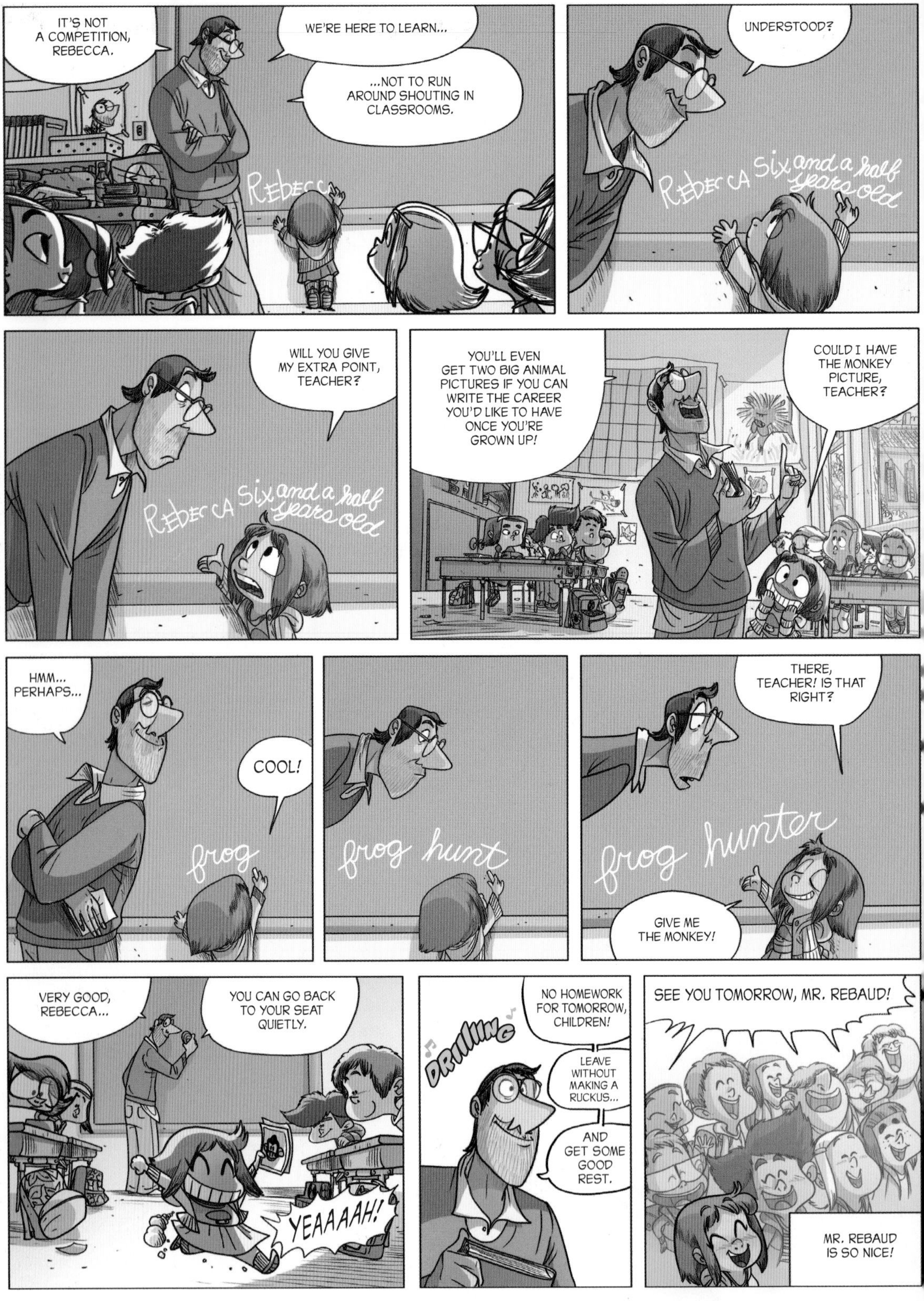
IT'S NOT A COMPETITION, REBECCA.
WE'RE HERE TO LEARN...
...NOT TO RUN AROUND SHOUTING IN CLASSROOMS.
REBECCA
UNDERSTOOD?
REBECCA Six and a half years old
WILL YOU GIVE MY EXTRA POINT, TEACHER?
REBECCA Six and a half years old
YOU'LL EVEN GET TWO BIG ANIMAL PICTURES IF YOU CAN WRITE THE CAREER YOU'D LIKE TO HAVE ONCE YOU'RE GROWN UP!
COULD I HAVE THE MONKEY PICTURE, TEACHER?
HMM... PERHAPS...
COOL!
frog
frog hunt
THERE, TEACHER! IS THAT RIGHT?
frog hunter
GIVE ME THE MONKEY!
VERY GOOD, REBECCA...
YOU CAN GO BACK TO YOUR SEAT QUIETLY.
YEAAAAH!
DRIIIING
NO HOMEWORK FOR TOMORROW, CHILDREN!
LEAVE WITHOUT MAKING A RUCKUS...
AND GET SOME GOOD REST.
SEE YOU TOMORROW, MR. REBAUD!
MR. REBAUD IS SO NICE!

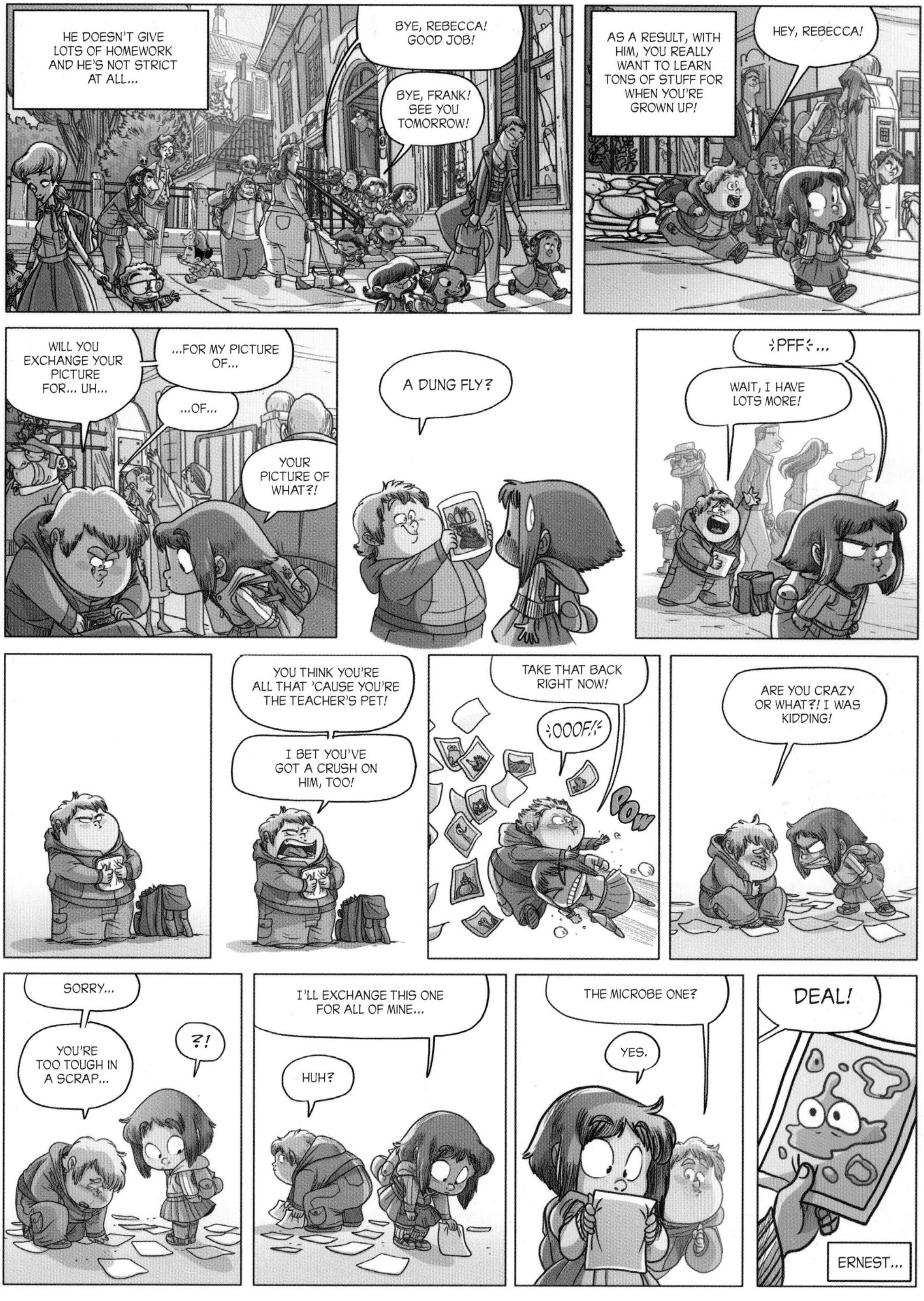
HE DOESN'T GIVE LOTS OF HOMEWORK AND HE'S NOT STRICT AT ALL...
BYE, REBECCA! GOOD JOB!
BYE, FRANK! SEE YOU TOMORROW!
AS A RESULT, WITH HIM, YOU REALLY WANT TO LEARN TONS OF STUFF FOR WHEN YOU'RE GROWN UP!
HEY, REBECCA!
WILL YOU EXCHANGE YOUR PICTURE FOR... UH...
...FOR MY PICTURE OF...
...OF...
YOUR PICTURE OF WHAT?!
A DUNG FLY?
PFF...
WAIT, I HAVE LOTS MORE!
YOU THINK YOU'RE ALL THAT 'CAUSE YOU'RE THE TEACHER'S PET!
I BET YOU'VE GOT A CRUSH ON HIM, TOO!
TAKE THAT BACK RIGHT NOW!
OOOF!
POW
ARE YOU CRAZY OR WHAT?! I WAS KIDDING!
SORRY...
YOU'RE TOO TOUGH IN A SCRAP...
?!
I'LL EXCHANGE THIS ONE FOR ALL OF MINE...
HUH?
THE MICROBE ONE?
YES.
DEAL!
ERNEST...

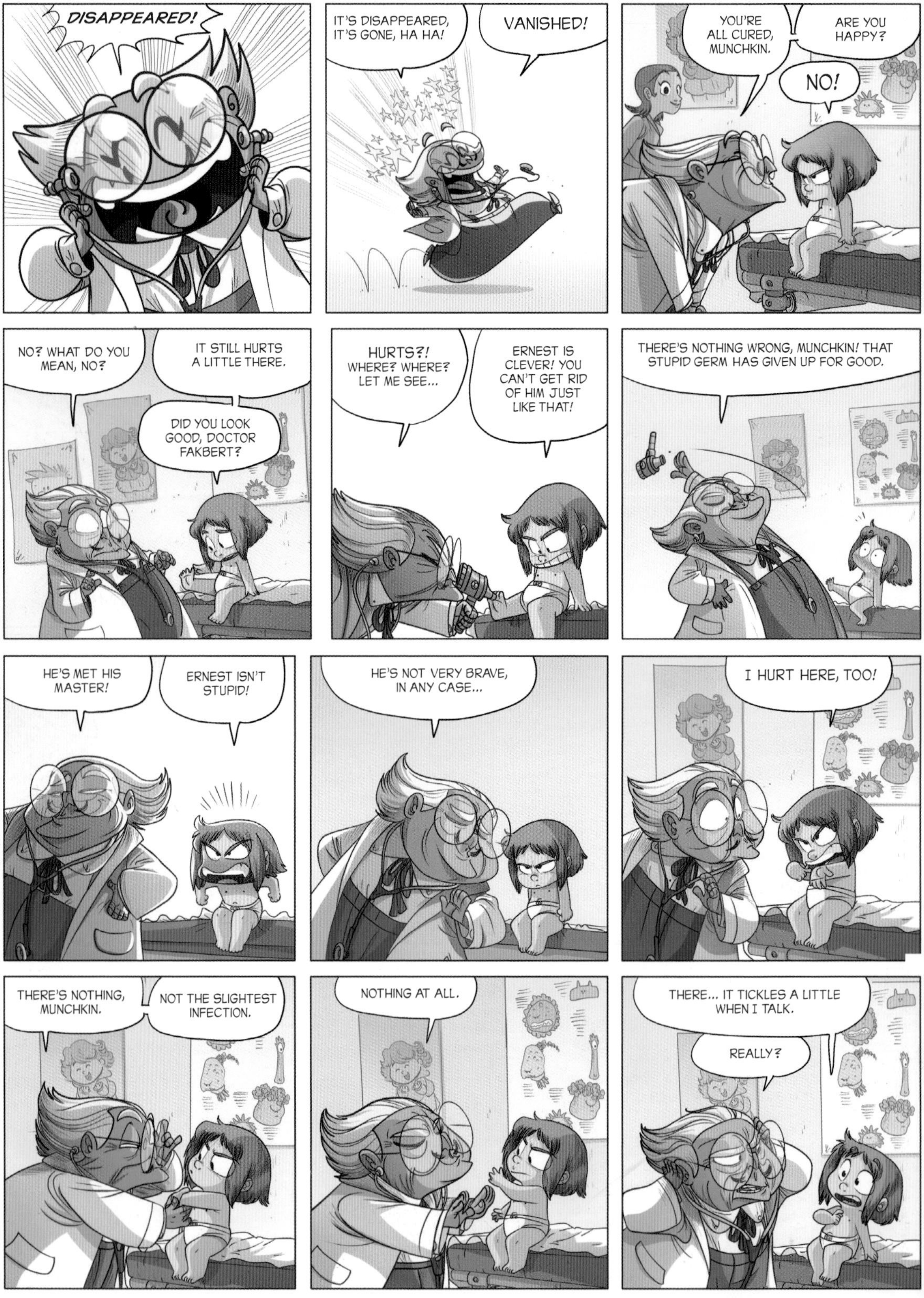

DISAPPEARED!
IT'S DISAPPEARED, IT'S GONE, HA HA!
VANISHED!
YOU'RE ALL CURED, MUNCHKIN.
ARE YOU HAPPY?
NO!
NO? WHAT DO YOU MEAN, NO?
IT STILL HURTS A LITTLE THERE.
DID YOU LOOK GOOD, DOCTOR FAKBERT?
HURTS?! WHERE? WHERE? LET ME SEE...
ERNEST IS CLEVER! YOU CAN'T GET RID OF HIM JUST LIKE THAT!
THERE'S NOTHING WRONG, MUNCHKIN! THAT STUPID GERM HAS GIVEN UP FOR GOOD.
HE'S MET HIS MASTER!
ERNEST ISN'T STUPID!
HE'S NOT VERY BRAVE, IN ANY CASE...
I HURT HERE, TOO!
THERE'S NOTHING, MUNCHKIN.
NOT THE SLIGHTEST INFECTION.
NOTHING AT ALL.
THERE... IT TICKLES A LITTLE WHEN I TALK.
REALLY?

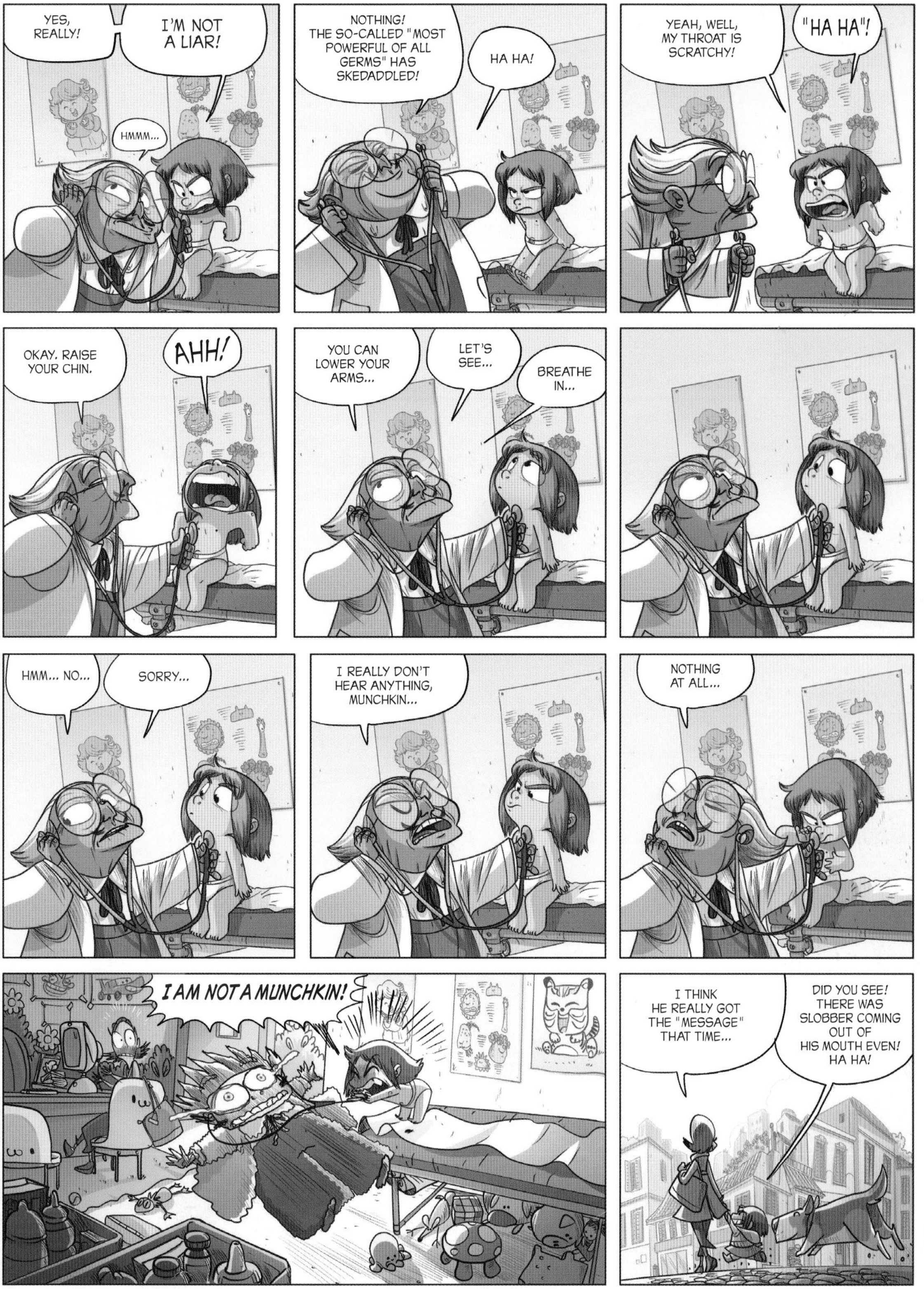
YES, REALLY!
I'M NOT A LIAR!
HMMM...
NOTHING! THE SO-CALLED "MOST POWERFUL OF ALL GERMS" HAS SKEDADDLED!
HA HA!
YEAH, WELL, MY THROAT IS SCRATCHY!
"HA HA"!
OKAY. RAISE YOUR CHIN.
AHH!
YOU CAN LOWER YOUR ARMS...
LET'S SEE...
BREATHE IN...
HMM... NO...
SORRY...
I REALLY DON'T HEAR ANYTHING, MUNCHKIN...
NOTHING AT ALL...
I AM NOT A MUNCHKIN!
I THINK HE REALLY GOT THE "MESSAGE" THAT TIME...
DID YOU SEE! THERE WAS SLOBBER COMING OUT OF HIS MOUTH EVEN! HA HA!

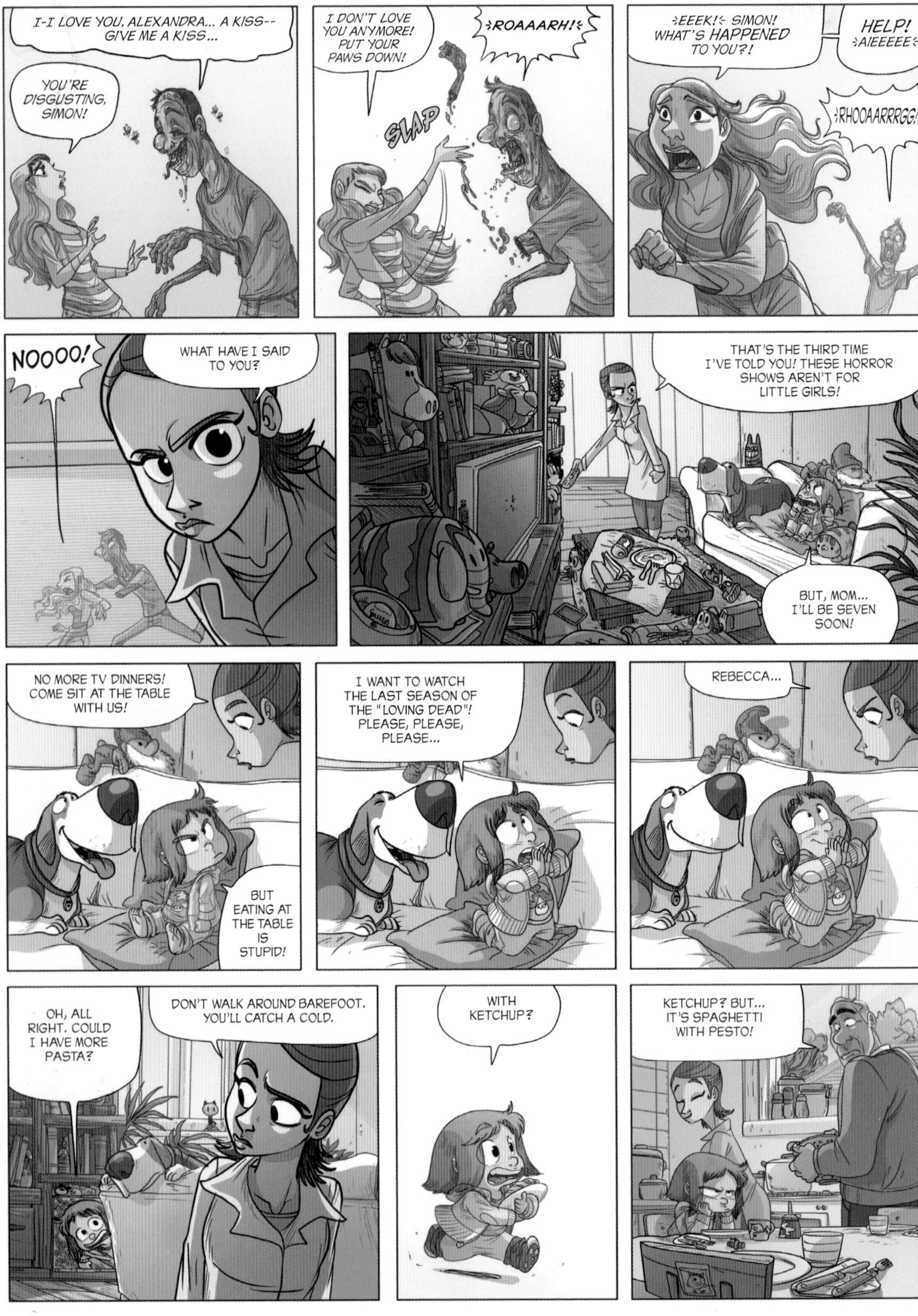
I-I LOVE YOU, ALEXANDRA... A KISS-- GIVE ME A KISS...
YOU'RE DISGUSTING, SIMON!
I DON'T LOVE YOU ANYMORE! PUT YOUR PAWS DOWN!
ROAAARH!
SLAP
EEEK! SIMON! WHAT'S HAPPENED TO YOU?!
HELP! AIEEEEE
RHOOAARRRGG!
NOOOO!
WHAT HAVE I SAID TO YOU?
THAT'S THE THIRD TIME I'VE TOLD YOU! THESE HORROR SHOWS AREN'T FOR LITTLE GIRLS!
BUT, MOM... I'LL BE SEVEN SOON!
NO MORE TV DINNERS! COME SIT AT THE TABLE WITH US!
BUT EATING AT THE TABLE IS STUPID!
I WANT TO WATCH THE LAST SEASON OF THE "LOVING DEAD"! PLEASE, PLEASE, PLEASE...
REBECCA...
OH, ALL RIGHT. COULD I HAVE MORE PASTA?
DON'T WALK AROUND BAREFOOT. YOU'LL CATCH A COLD.
WITH KETCHUP?
KETCHUP? BUT... IT'S SPAGHETTI WITH PESTO!

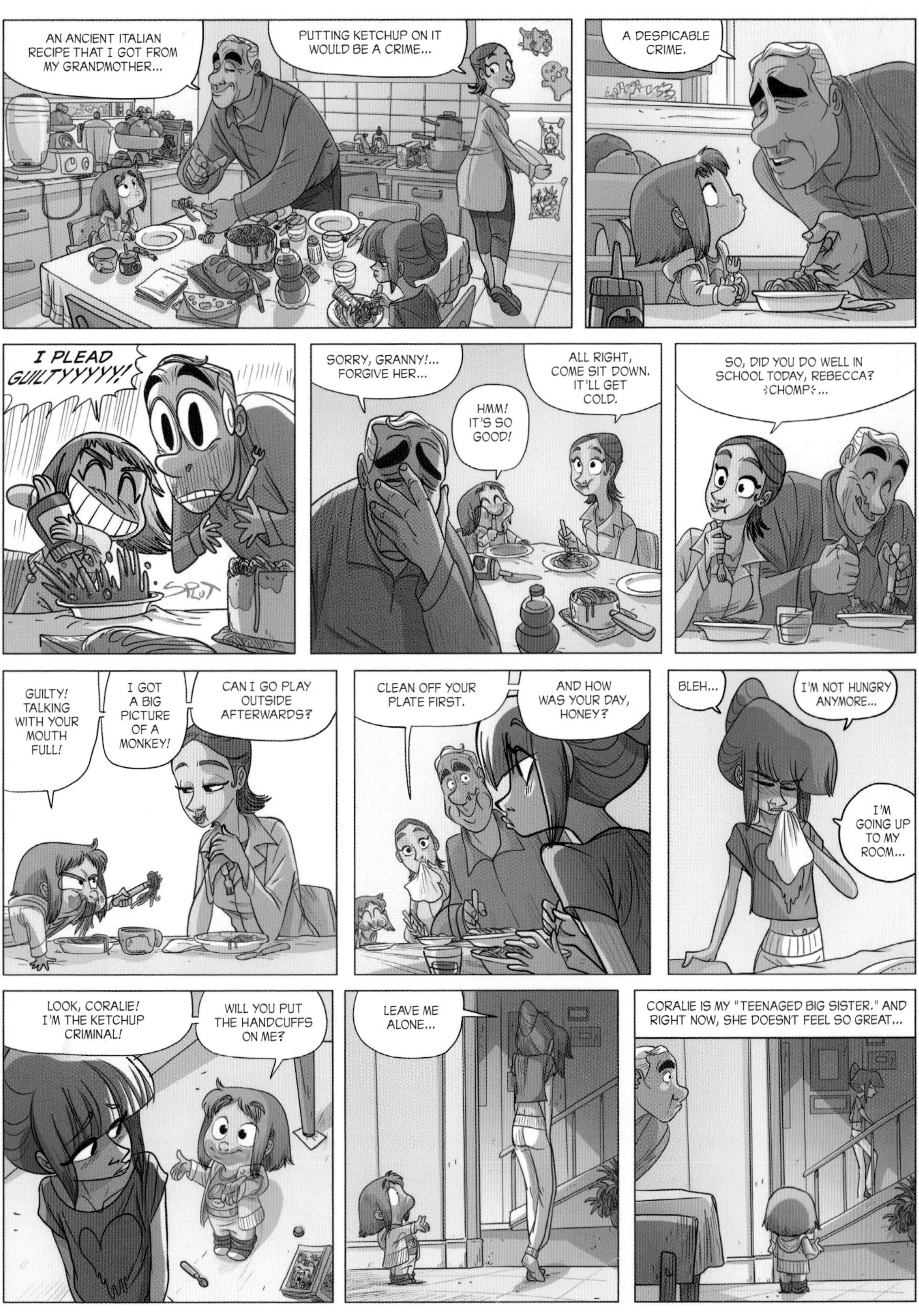
AN ANCIENT ITALIAN RECIPE THAT I GOT FROM MY GRANDMOTHER...
PUTTING KETCHUP ON IT WOULD BE A CRIME...
A DESPICABLE CRIME.
I PLEAD GUILTYYYYY!
SPLOT
SORRY, GRANNY!... FORGIVE HER...
HMM! IT'S SO GOOD!
ALL RIGHT, COME SIT DOWN. IT'LL GET COLD.
SO, DID YOU DO WELL IN SCHOOL TODAY, REBECCA? CHOMP...
GUILTY! TALKING WITH YOUR MOUTH FULL!
I GOT A BIG PICTURE OF A MONKEY!
CAN I GO PLAY OUTSIDE AFTERWARDS?
CLEAN OFF YOUR PLATE FIRST.
AND HOW WAS YOUR DAY, HONEY?
BLEH...
I'M NOT HUNGRY ANYMORE...
I'M GOING UP TO MY ROOM...
LOOK, CORALIE! I'M THE KETCHUP CRIMINAL!
WILL YOU PUT THE HANDCUFFS ON ME?
LEAVE ME ALONE...
CORALIE IS MY "TEENAGED BIG SISTER." AND RIGHT NOW, SHE DOESN'T FEEL SO GREAT...

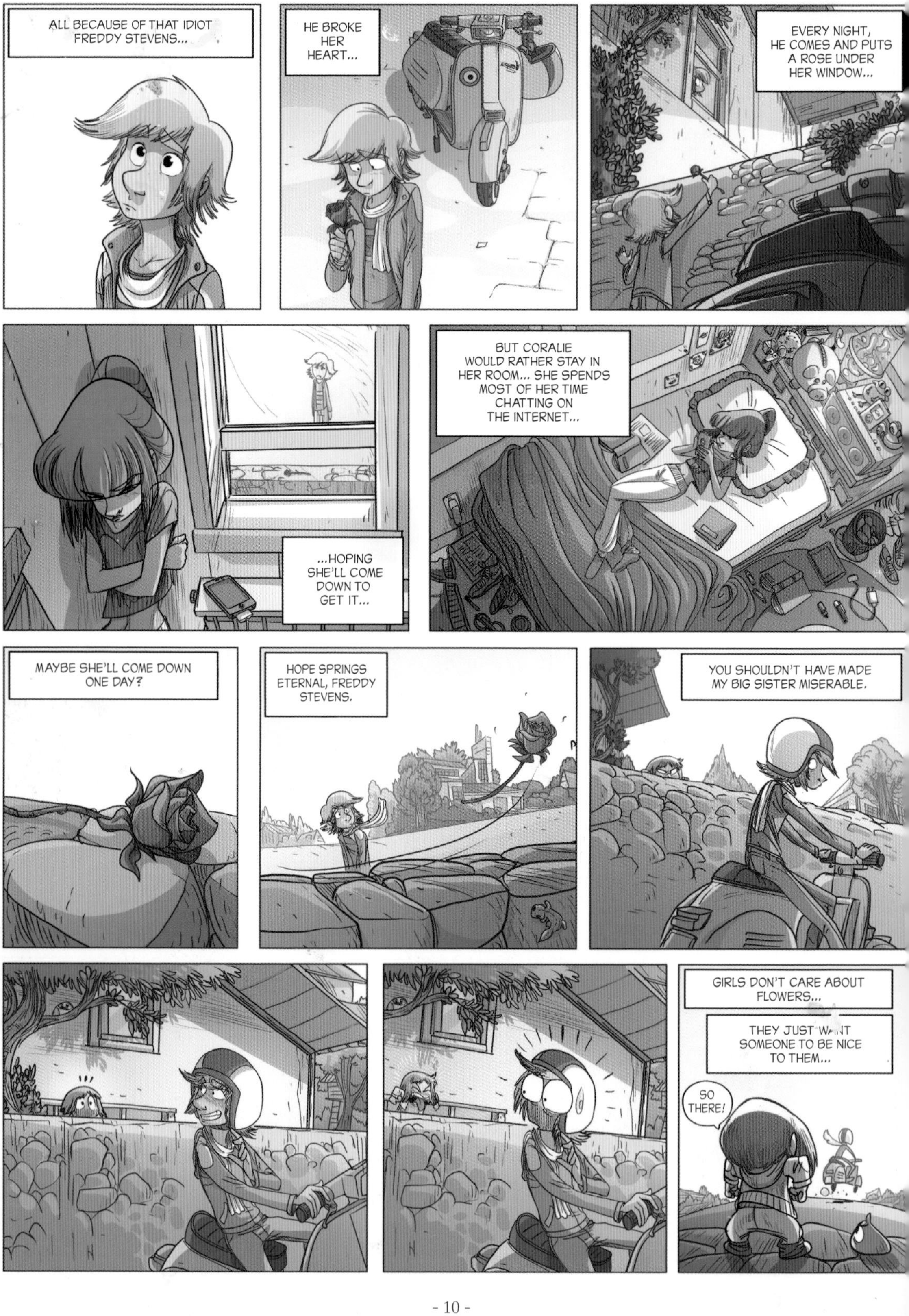
ALL BECAUSE OF THAT IDIOT FREDDY STEVENS...
HE BROKE HER HEART...
EVERY NIGHT, HE COMES AND PUTS A ROSE UNDER HER WINDOW...
...HOPING SHE'LL COME DOWN TO GET IT...
BUT CORALIE WOULD RATHER STAY IN HER ROOM... SHE SPENDS MOST OF HER TIME CHATTING ON THE INTERNET...
MAYBE SHE'LL COME DOWN ONE DAY?
HOPE SPRINGS ETERNAL, FREDDY STEVENS.
YOU SHOULDN'T HAVE MADE MY BIG SISTER MISERABLE.
GIRLS DON'T CARE ABOUT FLOWERS...
THEY JUST WANT SOMEONE TO BE NICE TO THEM...
SO THERE!

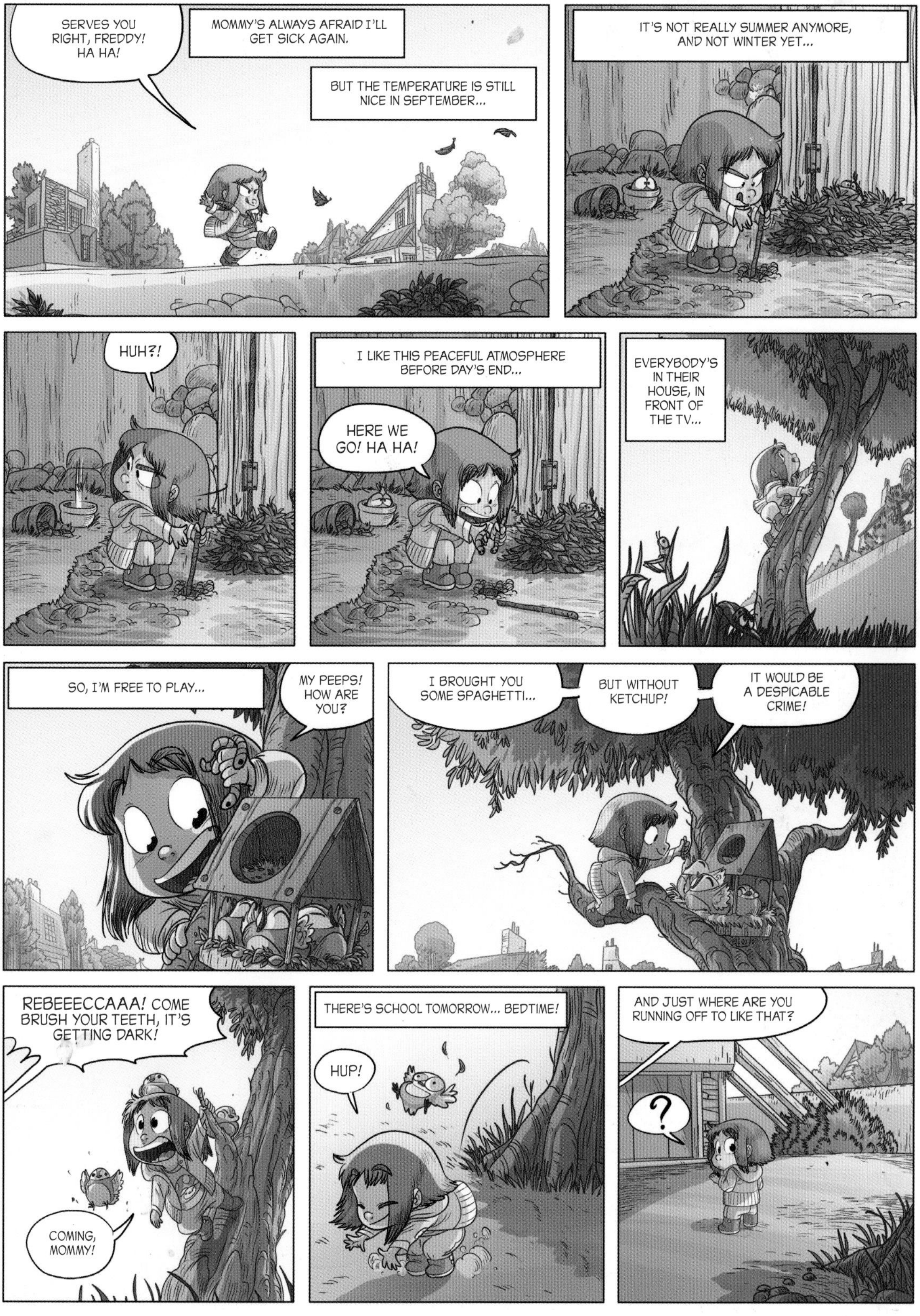
SERVES YOU RIGHT, FREDDY! HA HA!
MOMMY'S ALWAYS AFRAID I'LL GET SICK AGAIN.
BUT THE TEMPERATURE IS STILL NICE IN SEPTEMBER...
IT'S NOT REALLY SUMMER ANYMORE, AND NOT WINTER YET...
HUH?!
I LIKE THIS PEACEFUL ATMOSPHERE BEFORE DAY'S END...
HERE WE GO! HA HA!
EVERYBODY'S IN THEIR HOUSE, IN FRONT OF THE TV...
SO, I'M FREE TO PLAY...
MY PEEPS! HOW ARE YOU?
I BROUGHT YOU SOME SPAGHETTI...
BUT WITHOUT KETCHUP!
IT WOULD BE A DESPICABLE CRIME!
REBEEECCAAA! COME BRUSH YOUR TEETH, IT'S GETTING DARK!
COMING, MOMMY!
THERE'S SCHOOL TOMORROW... BEDTIME!
HUP!
AND JUST WHERE ARE YOU RUNNING OFF TO LIKE THAT?
?

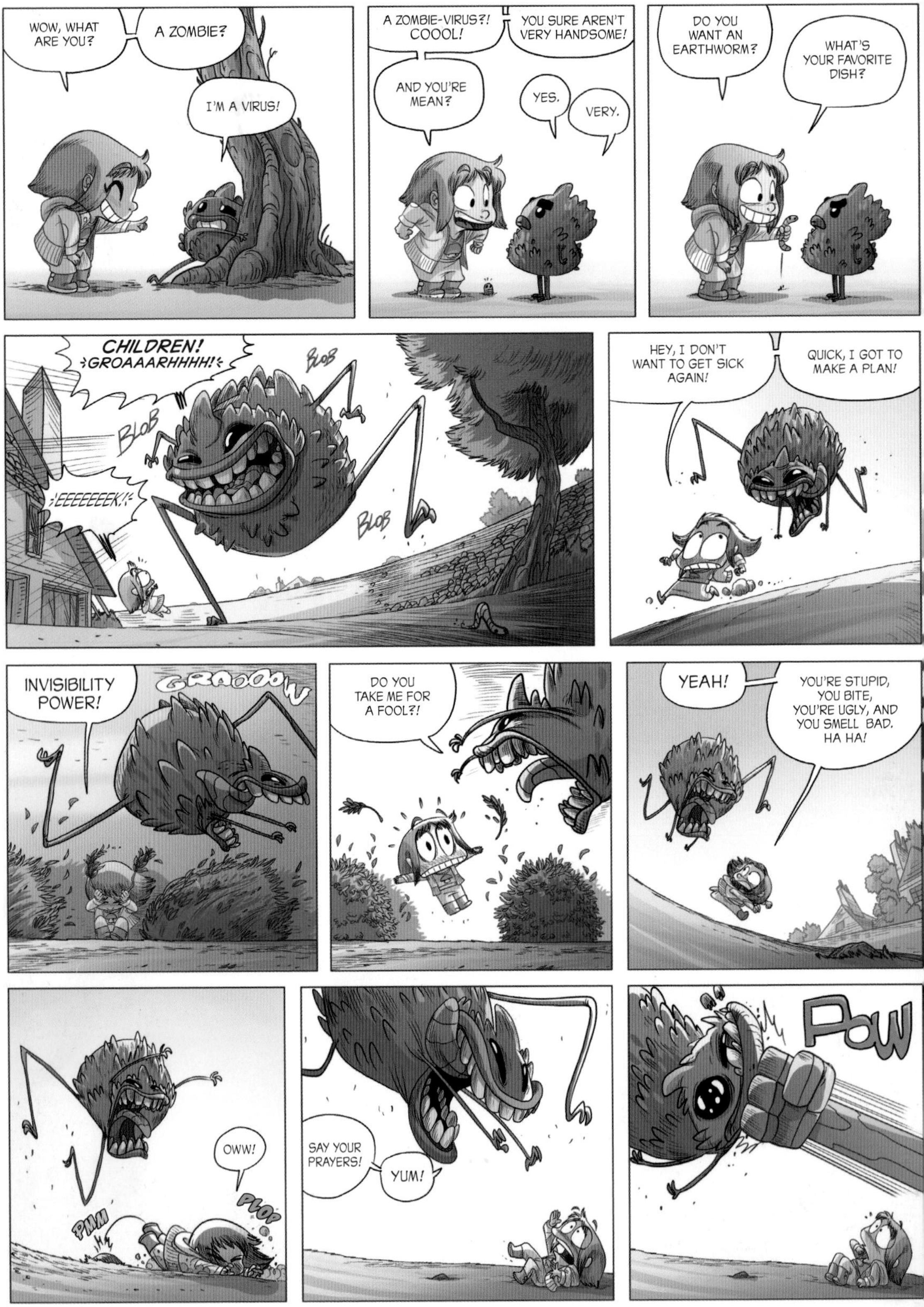
WOW, WHAT ARE YOU?
A ZOMBIE?
I'M A VIRUS!
A ZOMBIE-VIRUS?! COOOL!
YOU SURE AREN'T VERY HANDSOME!
AND YOU'RE MEAN?
YES.
VERY.
DO YOU WANT AN EARTHWORM?
WHAT'S YOUR FAVORITE DISH?
CHILDREN! GROAAARHHHH!
BLOB
BLOB
EEEEEEEK!
BLOB
HEY, I DON'T WANT TO GET SICK AGAIN!
QUICK, I GOT TO MAKE A PLAN!
INVISIBILITY POWER!
GRAOOOW
DO YOU TAKE ME FOR A FOOL?!
YEAH!
YOU'RE STUPID, YOU BITE, YOU'RE UGLY, AND YOU SMELL BAD. HA HA!
OWW!
PLOP
SAY YOUR PRAYERS!
YUM!
POW

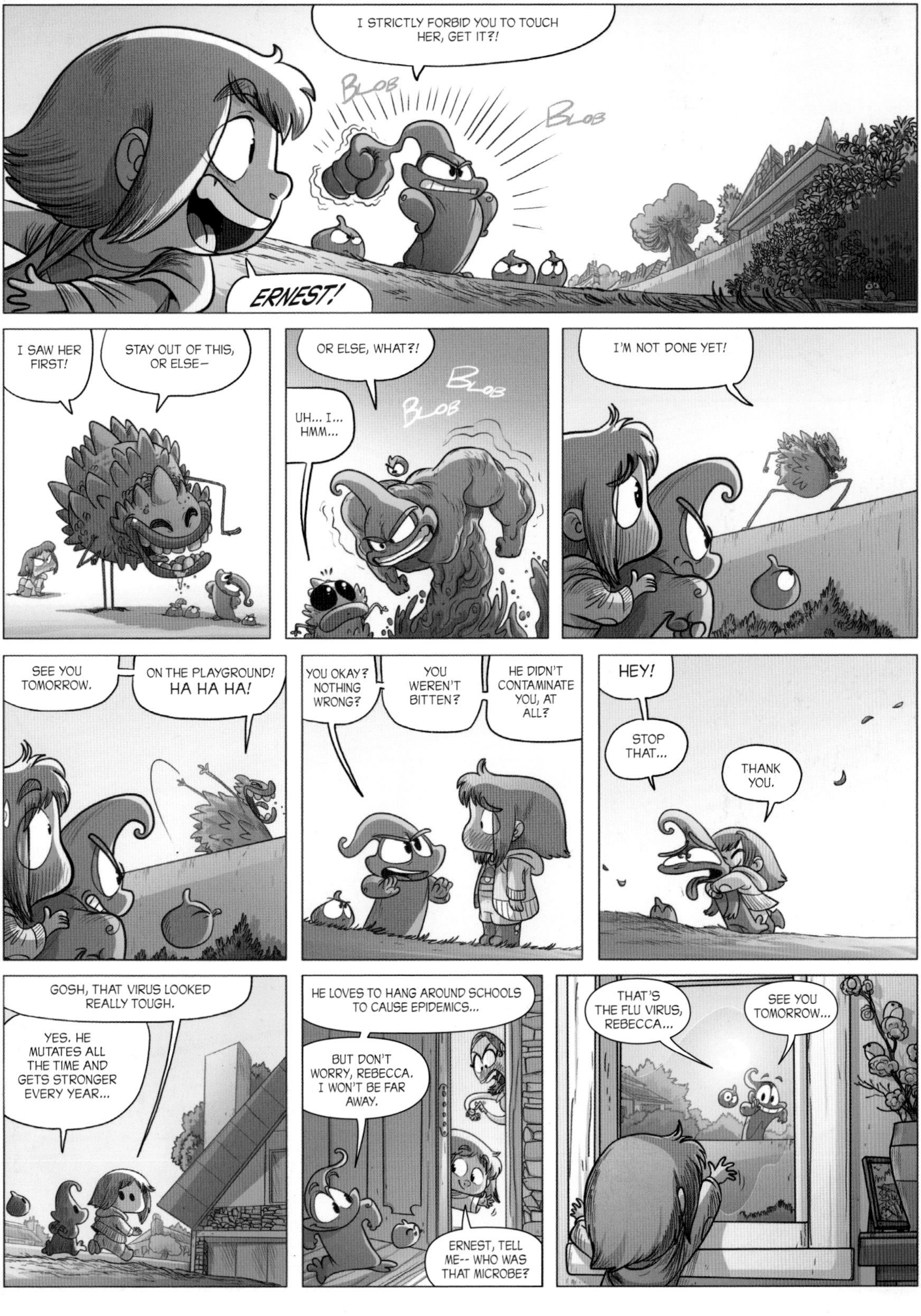
I STRICTLY FORBID YOU TO TOUCH HER, GET IT?!
BLOB
BLOB
ERNEST!
I SAW HER FIRST!
STAY OUT OF THIS, OR ELSE–
OR ELSE, WHAT?!
BLOB
BLOB
UH... I... HMM...
I'M NOT DONE YET!
SEE YOU TOMORROW.
ON THE PLAYGROUND! HA HA HA!
YOU OKAY? NOTHING WRONG?
YOU WEREN'T BITTEN?
HE DIDN'T CONTAMINATE YOU, AT ALL?
HEY!
STOP THAT...
THANK YOU.
GOSH, THAT VIRUS LOOKED REALLY TOUGH.
YES. HE MUTATES ALL THE TIME AND GETS STRONGER EVERY YEAR...
HE LOVES TO HANG AROUND SCHOOLS TO CAUSE EPIDEMICS...
BUT DON'T WORRY, REBECCA. I WON'T BE FAR AWAY.
ERNEST, TELL ME-- WHO WAS THAT MICROBE?
THAT'S THE FLU VIRUS, REBECCA...
SEE YOU TOMORROW...

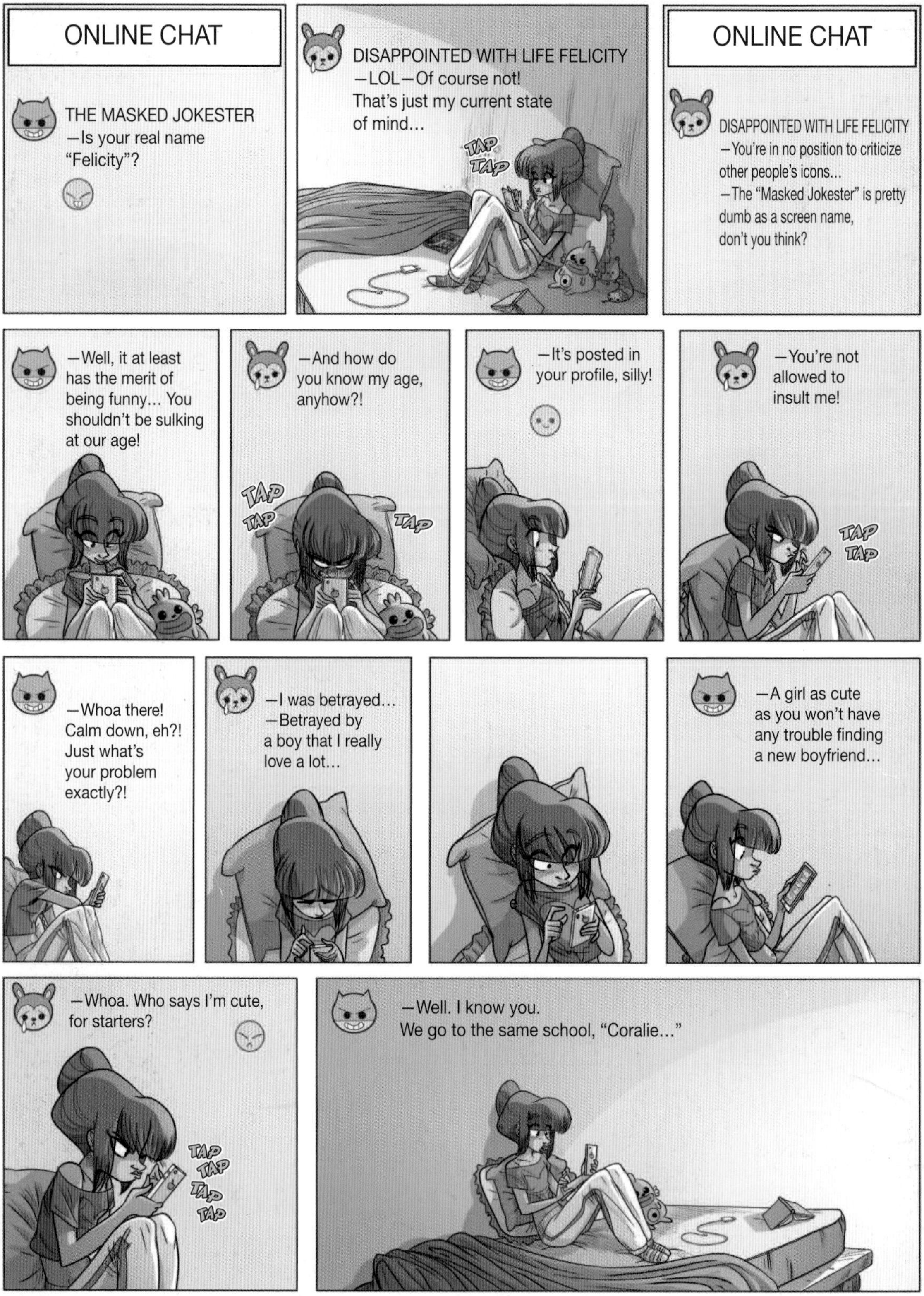
ONLINE CHAT
THE MASKED JOKESTER
—Is your real name "Felicity"?
DISAPPOINTED WITH LIFE FELICITY
—LOL—Of course not!
That's just my current state of mind...
TAP TAP
ONLINE CHAT
DISAPPOINTED WITH LIFE FELICITY
—You're in no position to criticize other people's icons...
—The "Masked Jokester" is pretty dumb as a screen name, don't you think?
—Well, it at least has the merit of being funny... You shouldn't be sulking at our age!
—And how do you know my age, anyhow?!
TAP TAP
TAP
—It's posted in your profile, silly!
—You're not allowed to insult me!
TAP TAP
—Whoa there! Calm down, eh?! Just what's your problem exactly?!
—I was betrayed...
—Betrayed by a boy that I really love a lot...
—A girl as cute as you won't have any trouble finding a new boyfriend...
—Whoa. Who says I'm cute, for starters?
TAP TAP TAP TAP
—Well. I know you.
We go to the same school, "Coralie..."

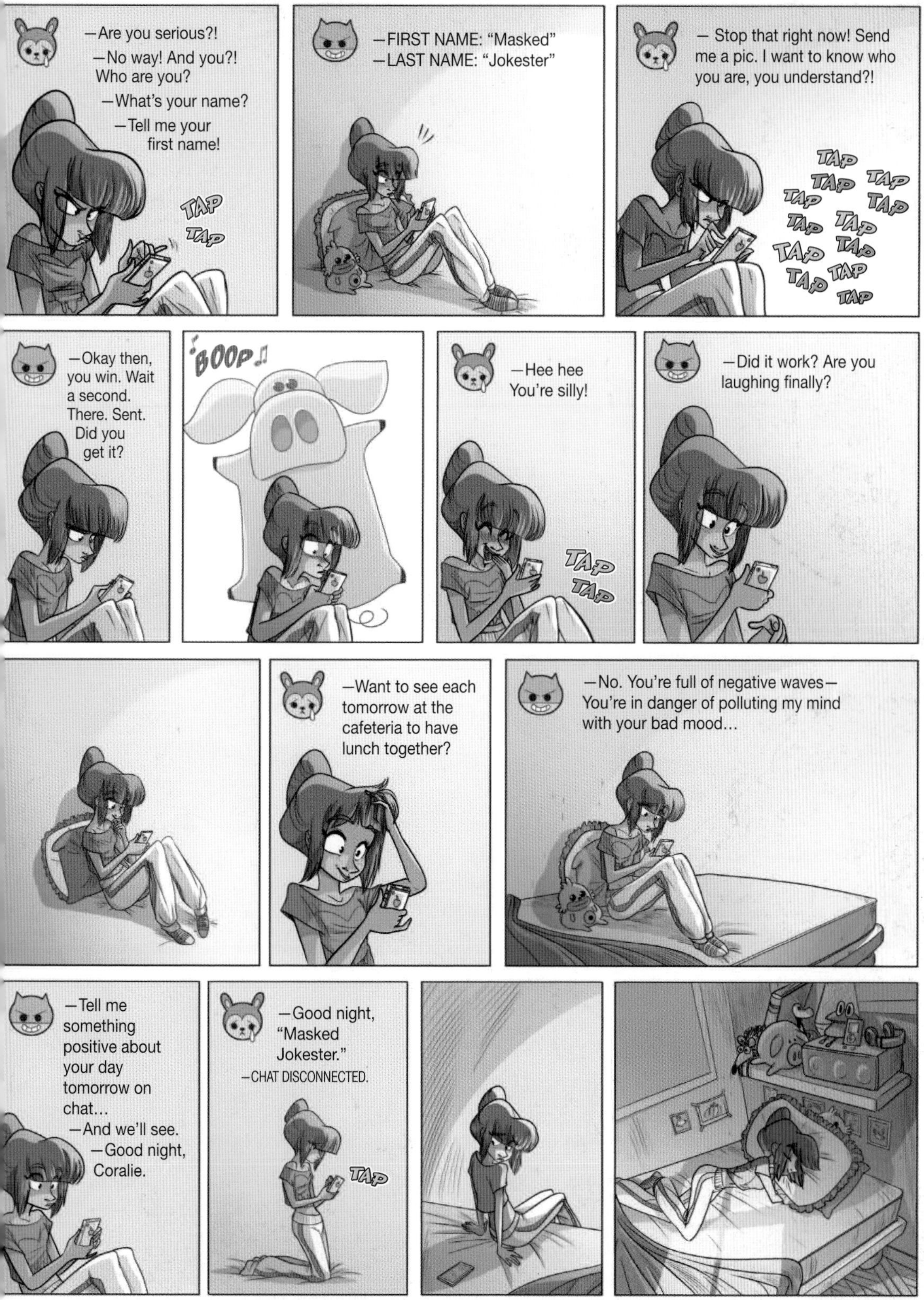
—Are you serious?!
—No way! And you?! Who are you?
—What's your name?
—Tell me your first name!
TAP
TAP
—FIRST NAME: "Masked"
—LAST NAME: "Jokester"
— Stop that right now! Send me a pic. I want to know who you are, you understand?!
TAP TAP TAP TAP TAP TAP TAP TAP TAP TAP TAP TAP
—Okay then, you win. Wait a second. There. Sent. Did you get it?
BOOP♫
—Hee hee You're silly!
TAP
TAP
—Did it work? Are you laughing finally?
—Want to see each tomorrow at the cafeteria to have lunch together?
—No. You're full of negative waves—You're in danger of polluting my mind with your bad mood…
—Tell me something positive about your day tomorrow on chat…
—And we'll see.
—Good night, Coralie.
—Good night, "Masked Jokester."
—CHAT DISCONNECTED.
TAP

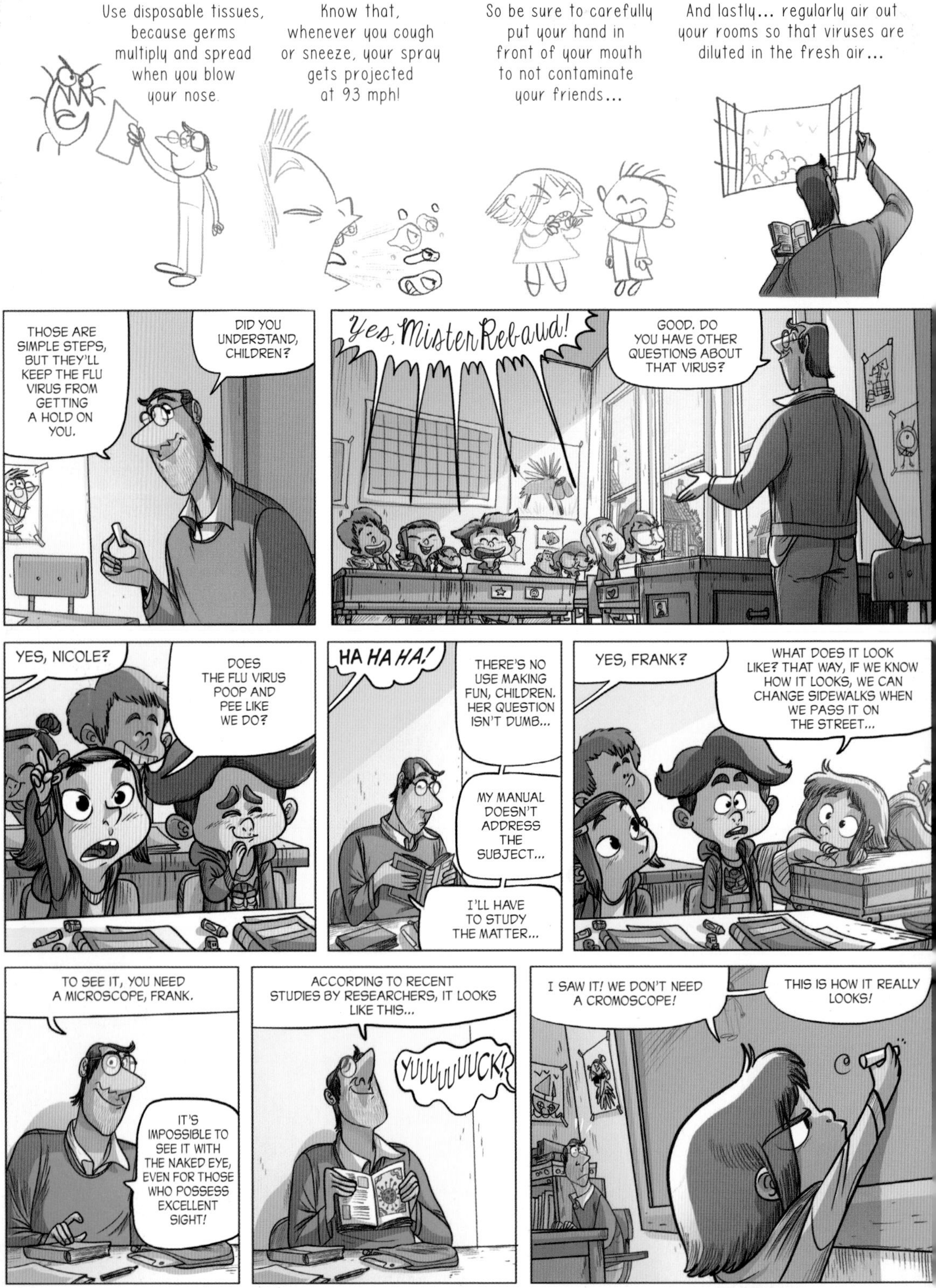

Use disposable tissues, because germs multiply and spread when you blow your nose.
Know that, whenever you cough or sneeze, your spray gets projected at 93 mph!
So be sure to carefully put your hand in front of your mouth to not contaminate your friends...
And lastly... regularly air out your rooms so that viruses are diluted in the fresh air...
THOSE ARE SIMPLE STEPS, BUT THEY'LL KEEP THE FLU VIRUS FROM GETTING A HOLD ON YOU.
DID YOU UNDERSTAND, CHILDREN?
Yes, Mister Rebaud!
GOOD. DO YOU HAVE OTHER QUESTIONS ABOUT THAT VIRUS?
YES, NICOLE?
DOES THE FLU VIRUS POOP AND PEE LIKE WE DO?
HA HA HA!
THERE'S NO USE MAKING FUN, CHILDREN. HER QUESTION ISN'T DUMB...
MY MANUAL DOESN'T ADDRESS THE SUBJECT...
I'LL HAVE TO STUDY THE MATTER...
YES, FRANK?
WHAT DOES IT LOOK LIKE? THAT WAY, IF WE KNOW HOW IT LOOKS, WE CAN CHANGE SIDEWALKS WHEN WE PASS IT ON THE STREET...
TO SEE IT, YOU NEED A MICROSCOPE, FRANK.
IT'S IMPOSSIBLE TO SEE IT WITH THE NAKED EYE, EVEN FOR THOSE WHO POSSESS EXCELLENT SIGHT!
ACCORDING TO RECENT STUDIES BY RESEARCHERS, IT LOOKS LIKE THIS...
YUUUUUUUCK!
I SAW IT! WE DON'T NEED A CROMOSCOPE!
THIS IS HOW IT REALLY LOOKS!

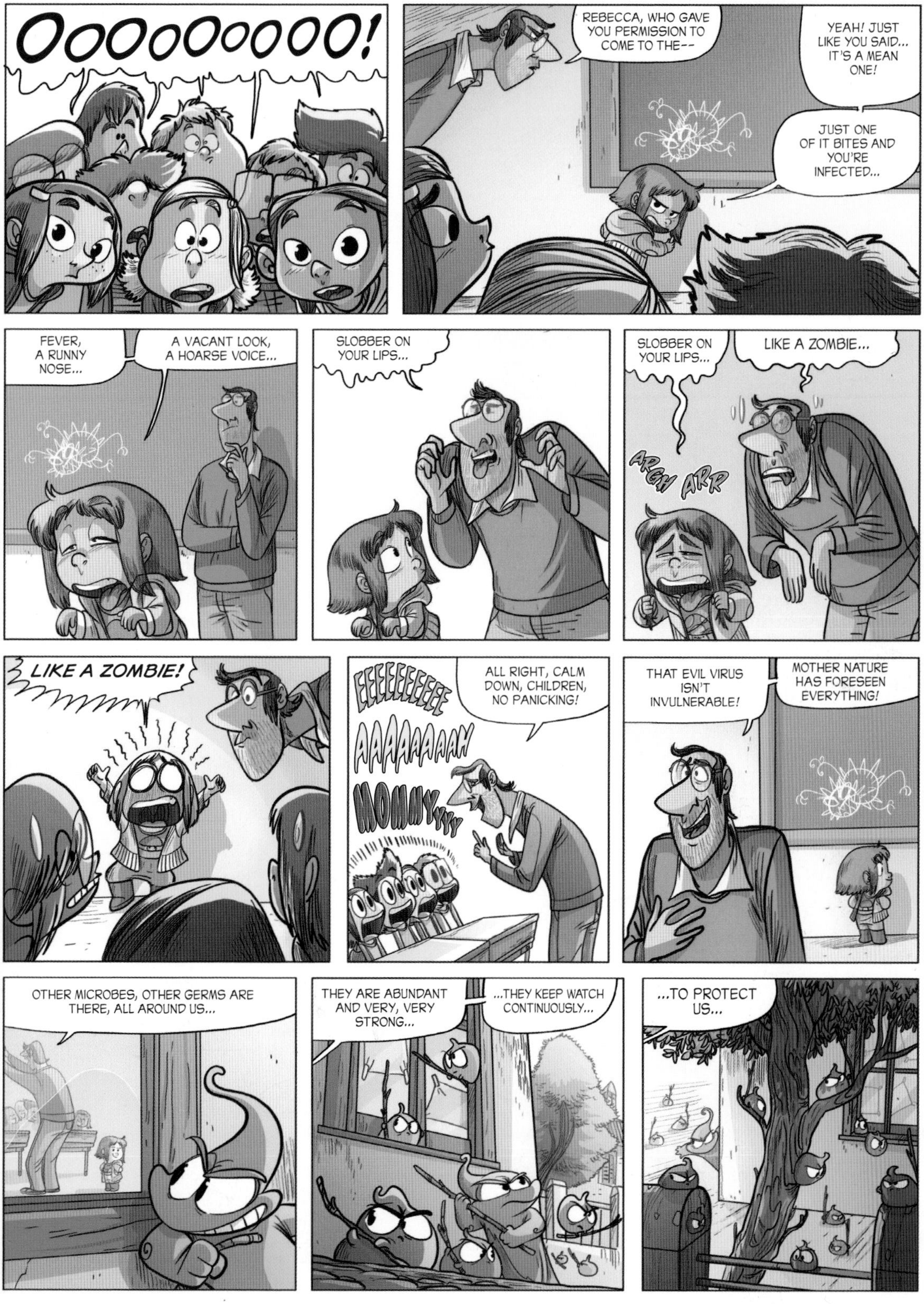
OOOOOOOOO!
REBECCA, WHO GAVE YOU PERMISSION TO COME TO THE--
YEAH! JUST LIKE YOU SAID... IT'S A MEAN ONE!
JUST ONE OF IT BITES AND YOU'RE INFECTED...
FEVER, A RUNNY NOSE...
A VACANT LOOK, A HOARSE VOICE...
SLOBBER ON YOUR LIPS...
SLOBBER ON YOUR LIPS...
LIKE A ZOMBIE...
ARGH ARR
LIKE A ZOMBIE!
EEEEEEEEEE
AAAAAAAAH
MOMMYYYY
ALL RIGHT, CALM DOWN, CHILDREN, NO PANICKING!
THAT EVIL VIRUS ISN'T INVULNERABLE!
MOTHER NATURE HAS FORESEEN EVERYTHING!
OTHER MICROBES, OTHER GERMS ARE THERE, ALL AROUND US...
THEY ARE ABUNDANT AND VERY, VERY STRONG...
...THEY KEEP WATCH CONTINUOUSLY...
...TO PROTECT US...

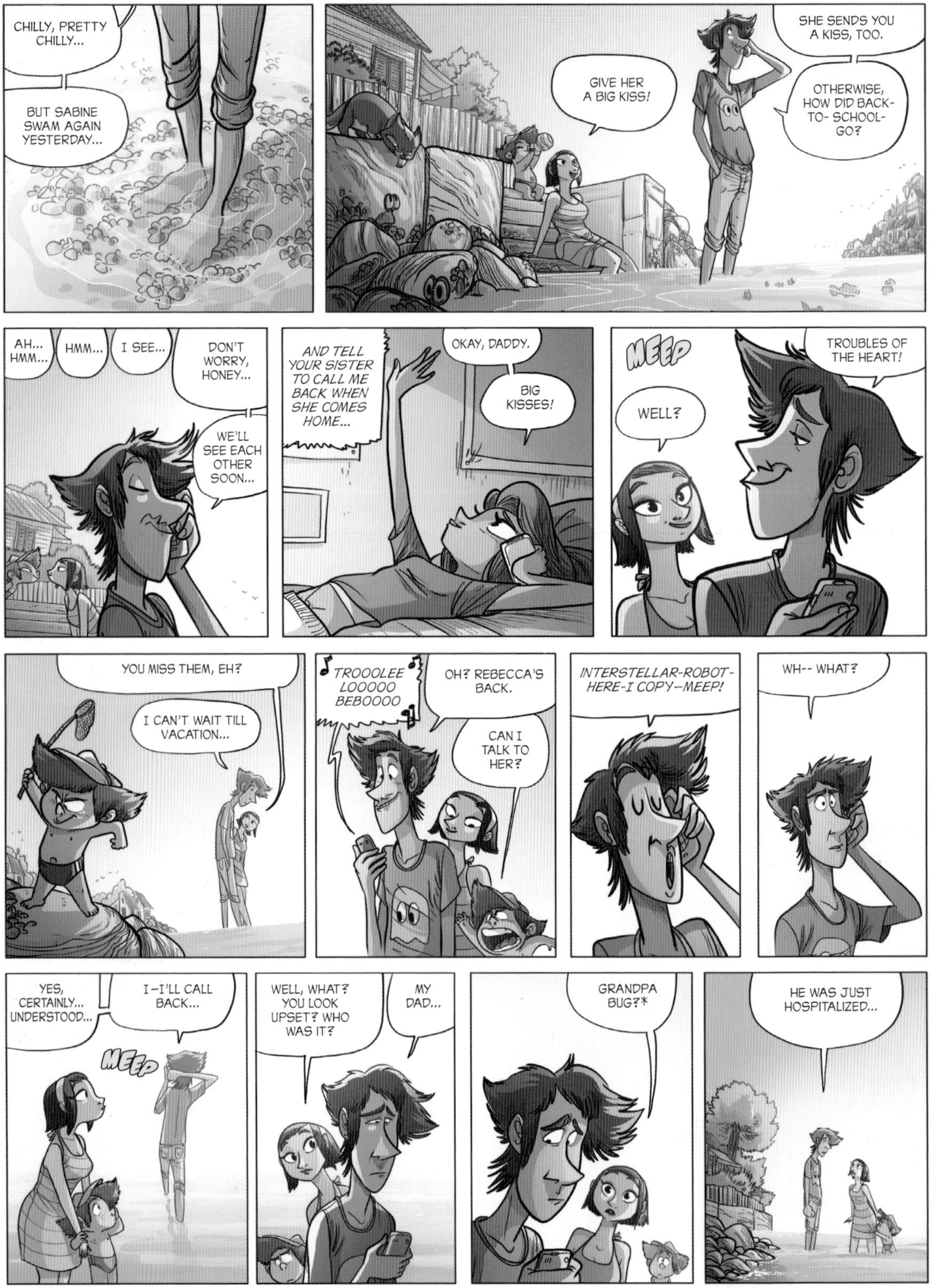
CHILLY, PRETTY CHILLY...
BUT SABINE SWAM AGAIN YESTERDAY...
GIVE HER A BIG KISS!
SHE SENDS YOU A KISS, TOO.
OTHERWISE, HOW DID BACK-TO- SCHOOL-GO?
AH... HMM...
HMM...
I SEE...
DON'T WORRY, HONEY...
WE'LL SEE EACH OTHER SOON...
AND TELL YOUR SISTER TO CALL ME BACK WHEN SHE COMES HOME...
OKAY, DADDY.
BIG KISSES!
MEEP
WELL?
TROUBLES OF THE HEART!
YOU MISS THEM, EH?
I CAN'T WAIT TILL VACATION...
TROOOLEE LOOOOO BEBOOOO
OH? REBECCA'S BACK.
CAN I TALK TO HER?
INTERSTELLAR-ROBOT-HERE-I COPY–MEEP!
WH-- WHAT?
YES, CERTAINLY... UNDERSTOOD...
I–I'LL CALL BACK...
MEEP
WELL, WHAT? YOU LOOK UPSET? WHO WAS IT?
MY DAD...
GRANDPA BUG?*
HE WAS JUST HOSPITALIZED...

*SEE ***ERNEST & REBECCA*** #3 "GRANDPA BUG."

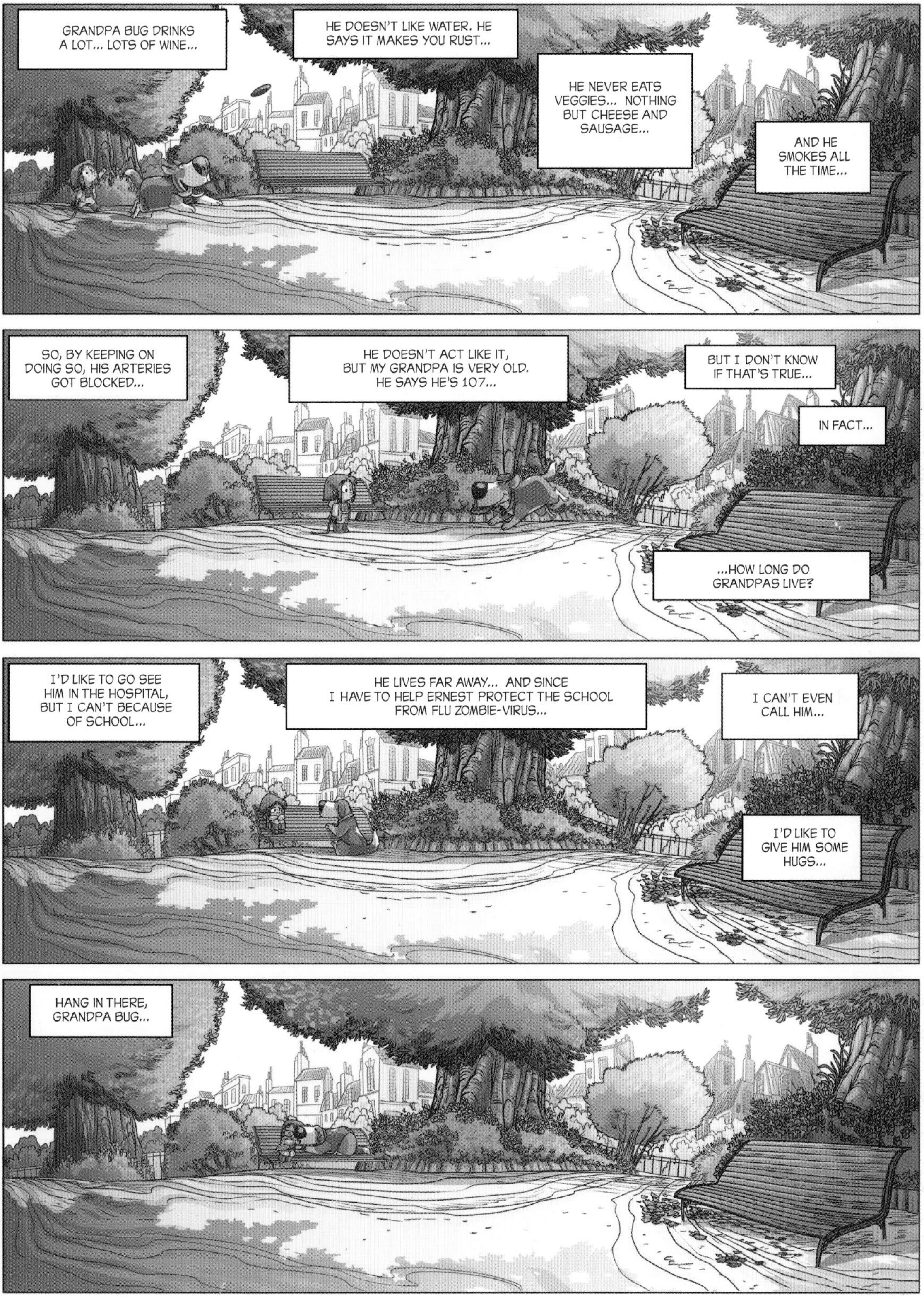
GRANDPA BUG DRINKS A LOT... LOTS OF WINE...
HE DOESN'T LIKE WATER. HE SAYS IT MAKES YOU RUST...
HE NEVER EATS VEGGIES... NOTHING BUT CHEESE AND SAUSAGE...
AND HE SMOKES ALL THE TIME...
SO, BY KEEPING ON DOING SO, HIS ARTERIES GOT BLOCKED...
HE DOESN'T ACT LIKE IT, BUT MY GRANDPA IS VERY OLD. HE SAYS HE'S 107...
BUT I DON'T KNOW IF THAT'S TRUE...
IN FACT...
...HOW LONG DO GRANDPAS LIVE?
I'D LIKE TO GO SEE HIM IN THE HOSPITAL, BUT I CAN'T BECAUSE OF SCHOOL...
HE LIVES FAR AWAY... AND SINCE I HAVE TO HELP ERNEST PROTECT THE SCHOOL FROM FLU ZOMBIE-VIRUS...
I CAN'T EVEN CALL HIM...
I'D LIKE TO GIVE HIM SOME HUGS...
HANG IN THERE, GRANDPA BUG...

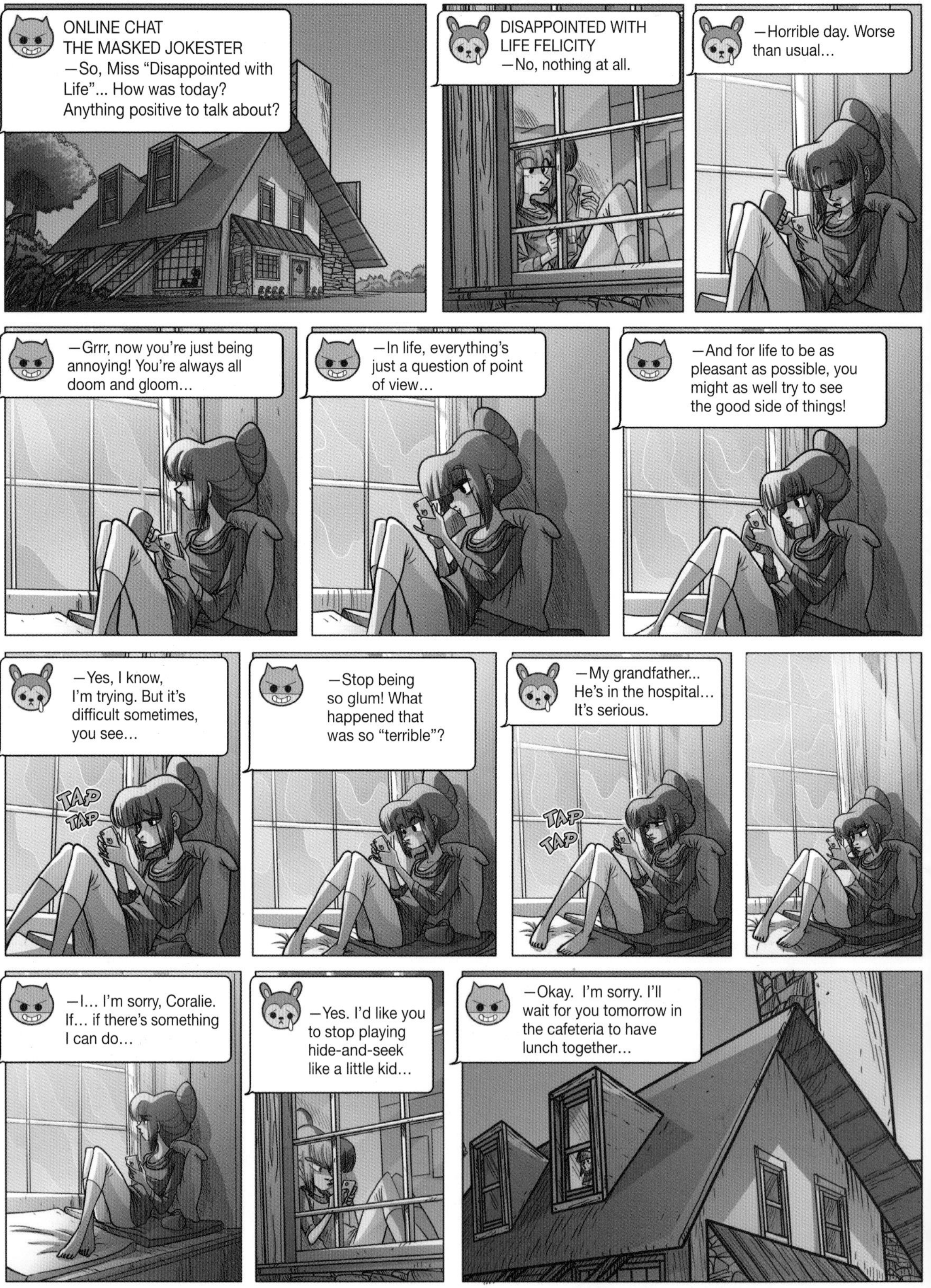
ONLINE CHAT
THE MASKED JOKESTER
—So, Miss "Disappointed with Life"... How was today? Anything positive to talk about?
DISAPPOINTED WITH LIFE FELICITY
—No, nothing at all.
—Horrible day. Worse than usual…
—Grrr, now you're just being annoying! You're always all doom and gloom…
—In life, everything's just a question of point of view…
—And for life to be as pleasant as possible, you might as well try to see the good side of things!
—Yes, I know, I'm trying. But it's difficult sometimes, you see…
TAP TAP
—Stop being so glum! What happened that was so "terrible"?
—My grandfather... He's in the hospital… It's serious.
TAP TAP
—I… I'm sorry, Coralie. If… if there's something I can do…
—Yes. I'd like you to stop playing hide-and-seek like a little kid…
—Okay. I'm sorry. I'll wait for you tomorrow in the cafeteria to have lunch together…

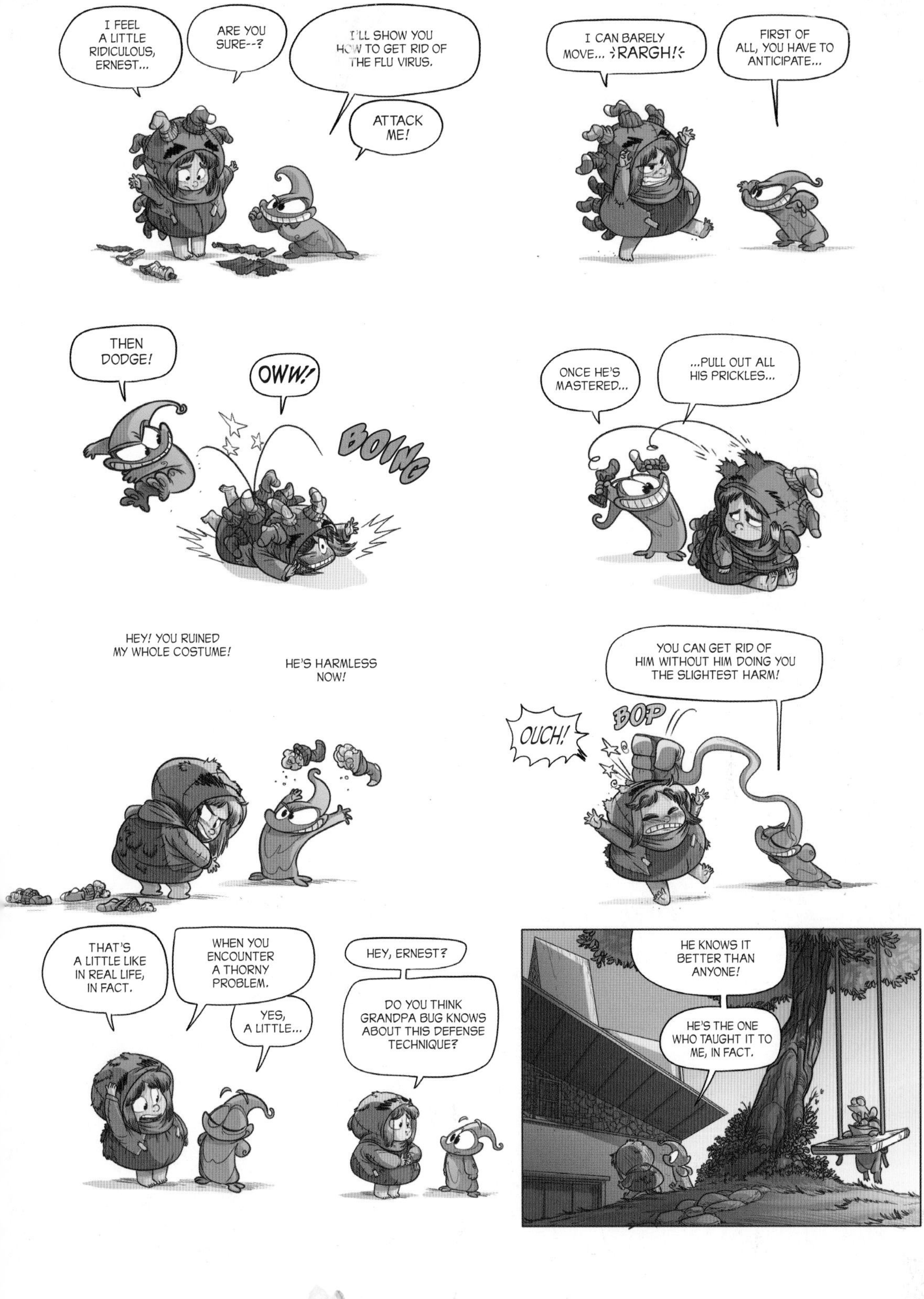
I FEEL A LITTLE RIDICULOUS, ERNEST...
ARE YOU SURE--?
I'LL SHOW YOU HOW TO GET RID OF THE FLU VIRUS.
ATTACK ME!
I CAN BARELY MOVE... RARGH!
FIRST OF ALL, YOU HAVE TO ANTICIPATE...
THEN DODGE!
OWW!
BOING
ONCE HE'S MASTERED...
...PULL OUT ALL HIS PRICKLES...
HEY! YOU RUINED MY WHOLE COSTUME!
HE'S HARMLESS NOW!
YOU CAN GET RID OF HIM WITHOUT HIM DOING YOU THE SLIGHTEST HARM!
OUCH!
BOP
THAT'S A LITTLE LIKE IN REAL LIFE, IN FACT.
WHEN YOU ENCOUNTER A THORNY PROBLEM.
YES, A LITTLE...
HEY, ERNEST?
DO YOU THINK GRANDPA BUG KNOWS ABOUT THIS DEFENSE TECHNIQUE?
HE KNOWS IT BETTER THAN ANYONE!
HE'S THE ONE WHO TAUGHT IT TO ME, IN FACT.

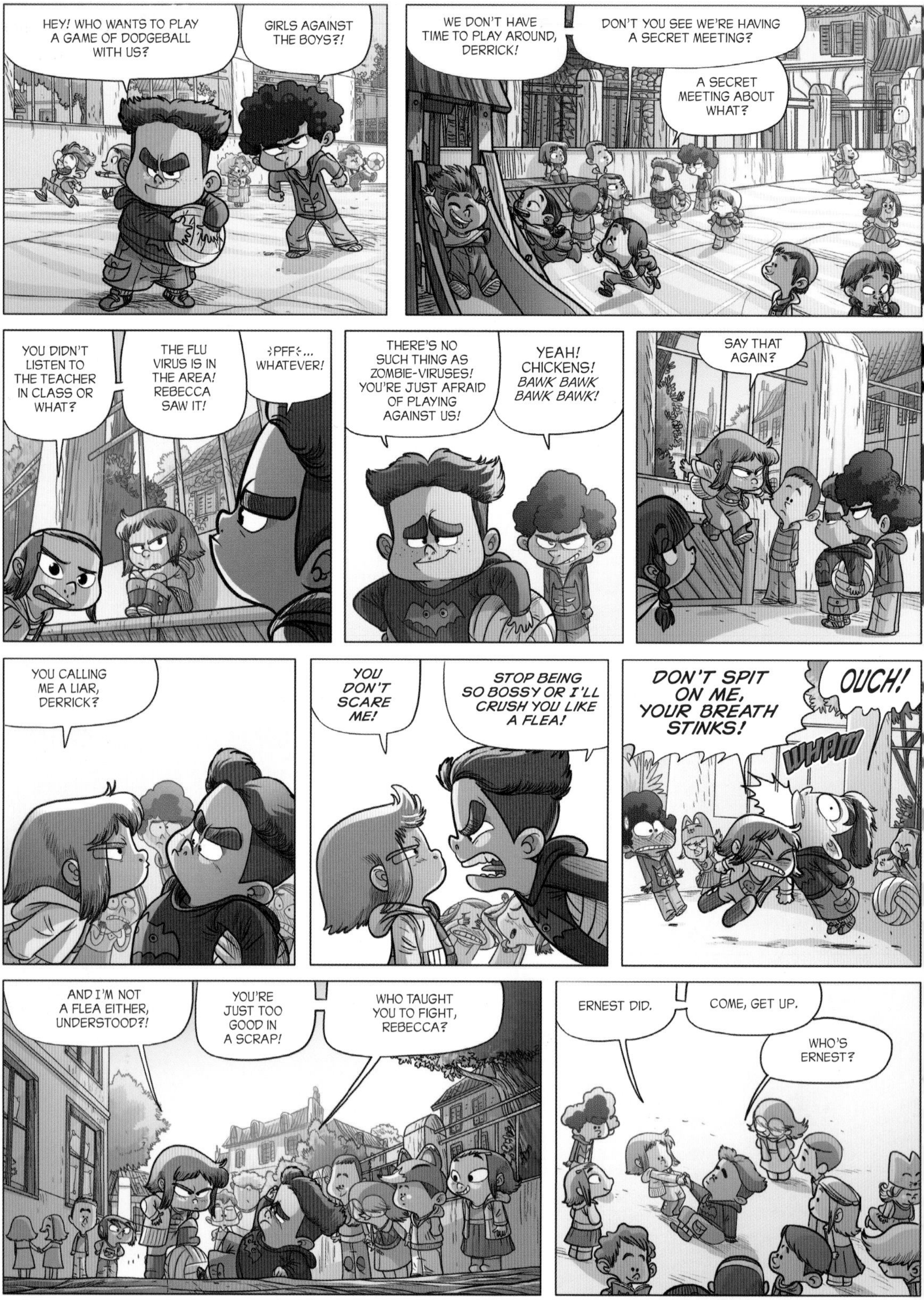
HEY! WHO WANTS TO PLAY A GAME OF DODGEBALL WITH US?
GIRLS AGAINST THE BOYS?!
WE DON'T HAVE TIME TO PLAY AROUND, DERRICK!
DON'T YOU SEE WE'RE HAVING A SECRET MEETING?
A SECRET MEETING ABOUT WHAT?
YOU DIDN'T LISTEN TO THE TEACHER IN CLASS OR WHAT?
THE FLU VIRUS IS IN THE AREA! REBECCA SAW IT!
PFF... WHATEVER!
THERE'S NO SUCH THING AS ZOMBIE-VIRUSES! YOU'RE JUST AFRAID OF PLAYING AGAINST US!
YEAH! CHICKENS! BAWK BAWK BAWK BAWK!
SAY THAT AGAIN?
YOU CALLING ME A LIAR, DERRICK?
YOU DON'T SCARE ME!
STOP BEING SO BOSSY OR I'LL CRUSH YOU LIKE A FLEA!
DON'T SPIT ON ME, YOUR BREATH STINKS!
OUCH!
WHAM
AND I'M NOT A FLEA EITHER, UNDERSTOOD?!
YOU'RE JUST TOO GOOD IN A SCRAP!
WHO TAUGHT YOU TO FIGHT, REBECCA?
ERNEST DID.
COME, GET UP.
WHO'S ERNEST?

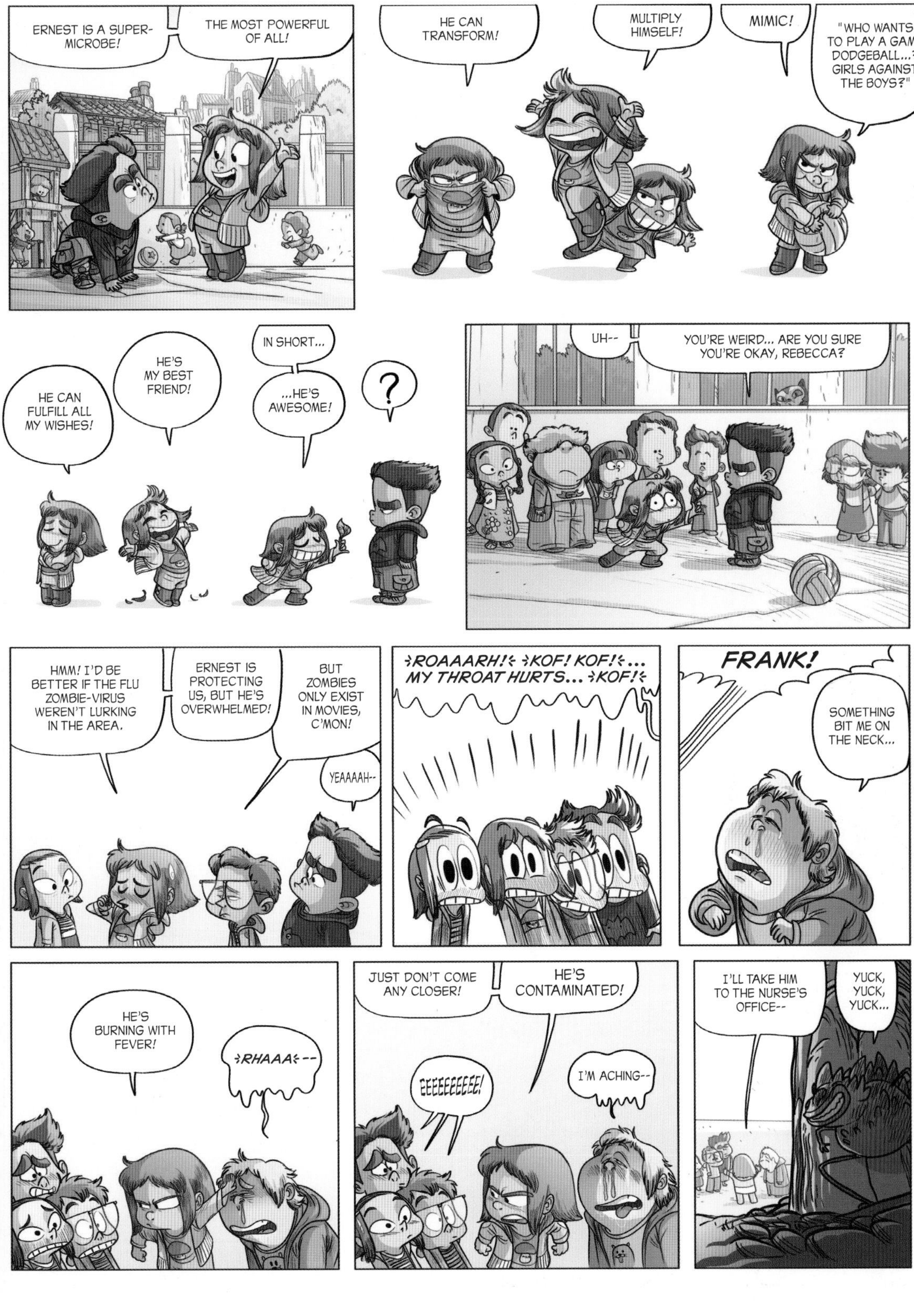
ERNEST IS A SUPER-MICROBE!
THE MOST POWERFUL OF ALL!
HE CAN TRANSFORM!
MULTIPLY HIMSELF!
MIMIC!
"WHO WANTS TO PLAY A GAME DODGEBALL...? GIRLS AGAINST THE BOYS?"
HE CAN FULFILL ALL MY WISHES!
HE'S MY BEST FRIEND!
IN SHORT...
...HE'S AWESOME!
?
UH--
YOU'RE WEIRD... ARE YOU SURE YOU'RE OKAY, REBECCA?
HMM! I'D BE BETTER IF THE FLU ZOMBIE-VIRUS WEREN'T LURKING IN THE AREA.
ERNEST IS PROTECTING US, BUT HE'S OVERWHELMED!
BUT ZOMBIES ONLY EXIST IN MOVIES, C'MON!
YEAAAAH--
ROAAARH! KOF! KOF!... MY THROAT HURTS... KOF!
FRANK!
SOMETHING BIT ME ON THE NECK...
HE'S BURNING WITH FEVER!
RHAAA--
JUST DON'T COME ANY CLOSER!
HE'S CONTAMINATED!
EEEEEEEEEE!
I'M ACHING--
I'LL TAKE HIM TO THE NURSE'S OFFICE--
YUCK, YUCK, YUCK...

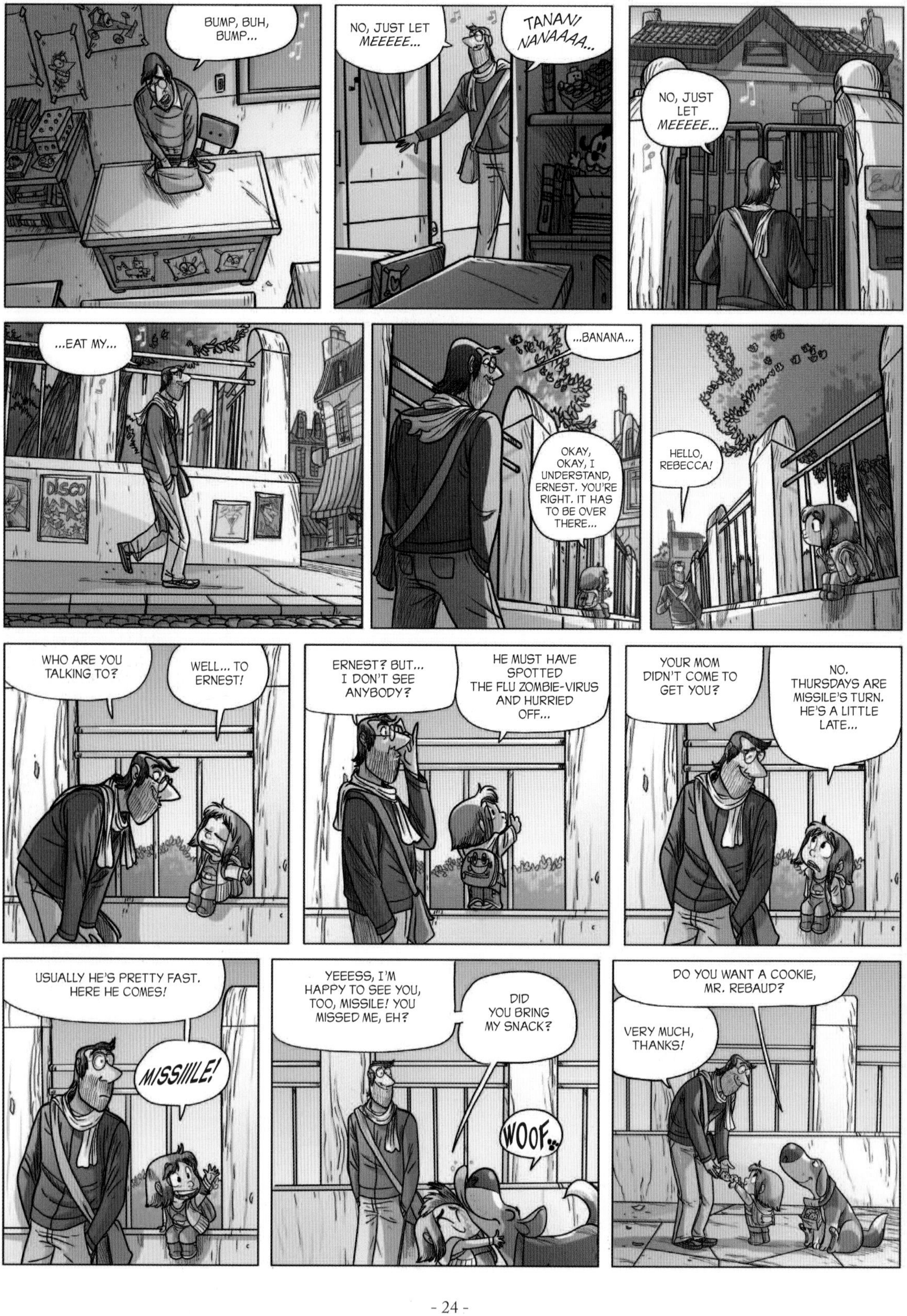
BUMP, BUH, BUMP...
NO, JUST LET MEEEEE...
TANAN! NANAAAA...
NO, JUST LET MEEEEE...
...EAT MY...
...BANANA...
OKAY, OKAY, I UNDERSTAND, ERNEST. YOU'RE RIGHT. IT HAS TO BE OVER THERE...
HELLO, REBECCA!
WHO ARE YOU TALKING TO?
WELL... TO ERNEST!
ERNEST? BUT... I DON'T SEE ANYBODY?
HE MUST HAVE SPOTTED THE FLU ZOMBIE-VIRUS AND HURRIED OFF...
YOUR MOM DIDN'T COME TO GET YOU?
NO. THURSDAYS ARE MISSILE'S TURN. HE'S A LITTLE LATE...
USUALLY HE'S PRETTY FAST. HERE HE COMES!
MISSIIILE!
YEEEESS, I'M HAPPY TO SEE YOU, TOO, MISSILE! YOU MISSED ME, EH?
DID YOU BRING MY SNACK?
WOOF
DO YOU WANT A COOKIE, MR. REBAUD?
VERY MUCH, THANKS!

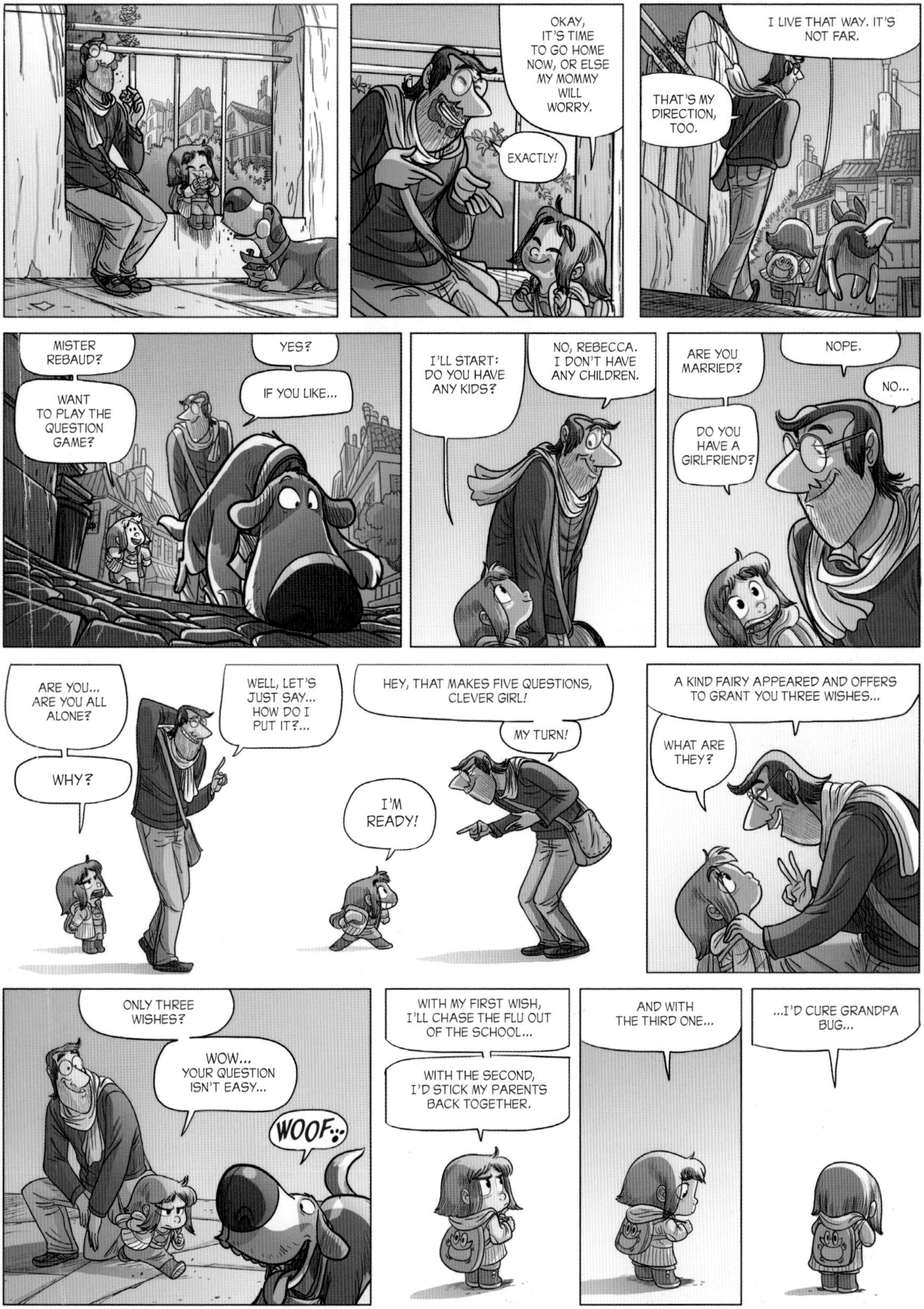
OKAY, IT'S TIME TO GO HOME NOW, OR ELSE MY MOMMY WILL WORRY.
EXACTLY!
I LIVE THAT WAY. IT'S NOT FAR.
THAT'S MY DIRECTION, TOO.
MISTER REBAUD?
YES?
WANT TO PLAY THE QUESTION GAME?
IF YOU LIKE...
I'LL START: DO YOU HAVE ANY KIDS?
NO, REBECCA. I DON'T HAVE ANY CHILDREN.
ARE YOU MARRIED?
NOPE.
DO YOU HAVE A GIRLFRIEND?
NO...
ARE YOU... ARE YOU ALL ALONE?
WELL, LET'S JUST SAY... HOW DO I PUT IT?...
WHY?
HEY, THAT MAKES FIVE QUESTIONS, CLEVER GIRL!
MY TURN!
I'M READY!
A KIND FAIRY APPEARED AND OFFERS TO GRANT YOU THREE WISHES...
WHAT ARE THEY?
ONLY THREE WISHES?
WOW... YOUR QUESTION ISN'T EASY...
WOOF
WITH MY FIRST WISH, I'LL CHASE THE FLU OUT OF THE SCHOOL...
WITH THE SECOND, I'D STICK MY PARENTS BACK TOGETHER.
AND WITH THE THIRD ONE...
...I'D CURE GRANDPA BUG...

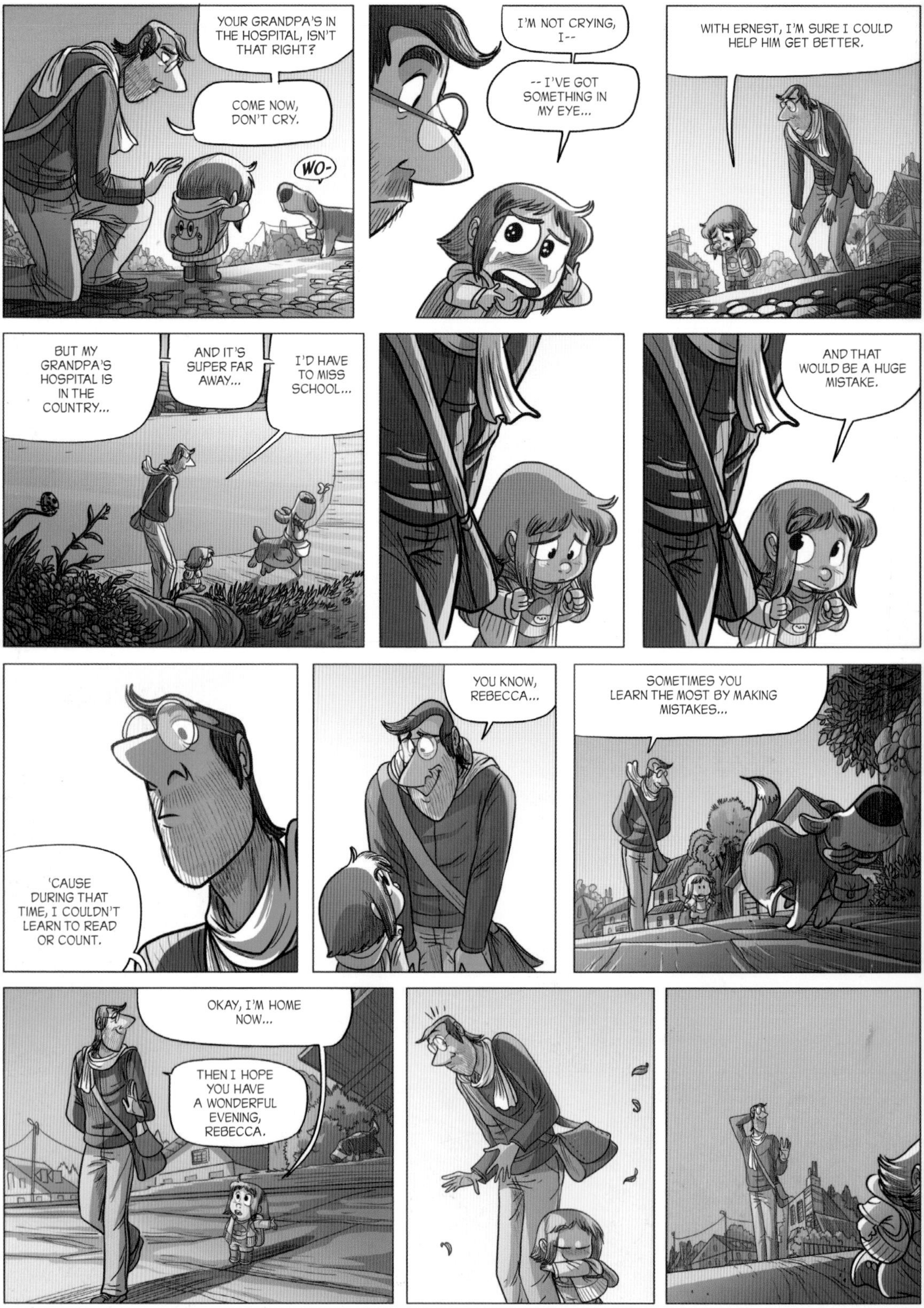
YOUR GRANDPA'S IN THE HOSPITAL, ISN'T THAT RIGHT?
COME NOW, DON'T CRY.
WO-
I'M NOT CRYING, I--
-- I'VE GOT SOMETHING IN MY EYE...
WITH ERNEST, I'M SURE I COULD HELP HIM GET BETTER.
BUT MY GRANDPA'S HOSPITAL IS IN THE COUNTRY...
AND IT'S SUPER FAR AWAY...
I'D HAVE TO MISS SCHOOL...
AND THAT WOULD BE A HUGE MISTAKE.
'CAUSE DURING THAT TIME, I COULDN'T LEARN TO READ OR COUNT.
YOU KNOW, REBECCA...
SOMETIMES YOU LEARN THE MOST BY MAKING MISTAKES...
OKAY, I'M HOME NOW...
THEN I HOPE YOU HAVE A WONDERFUL EVENING, REBECCA.

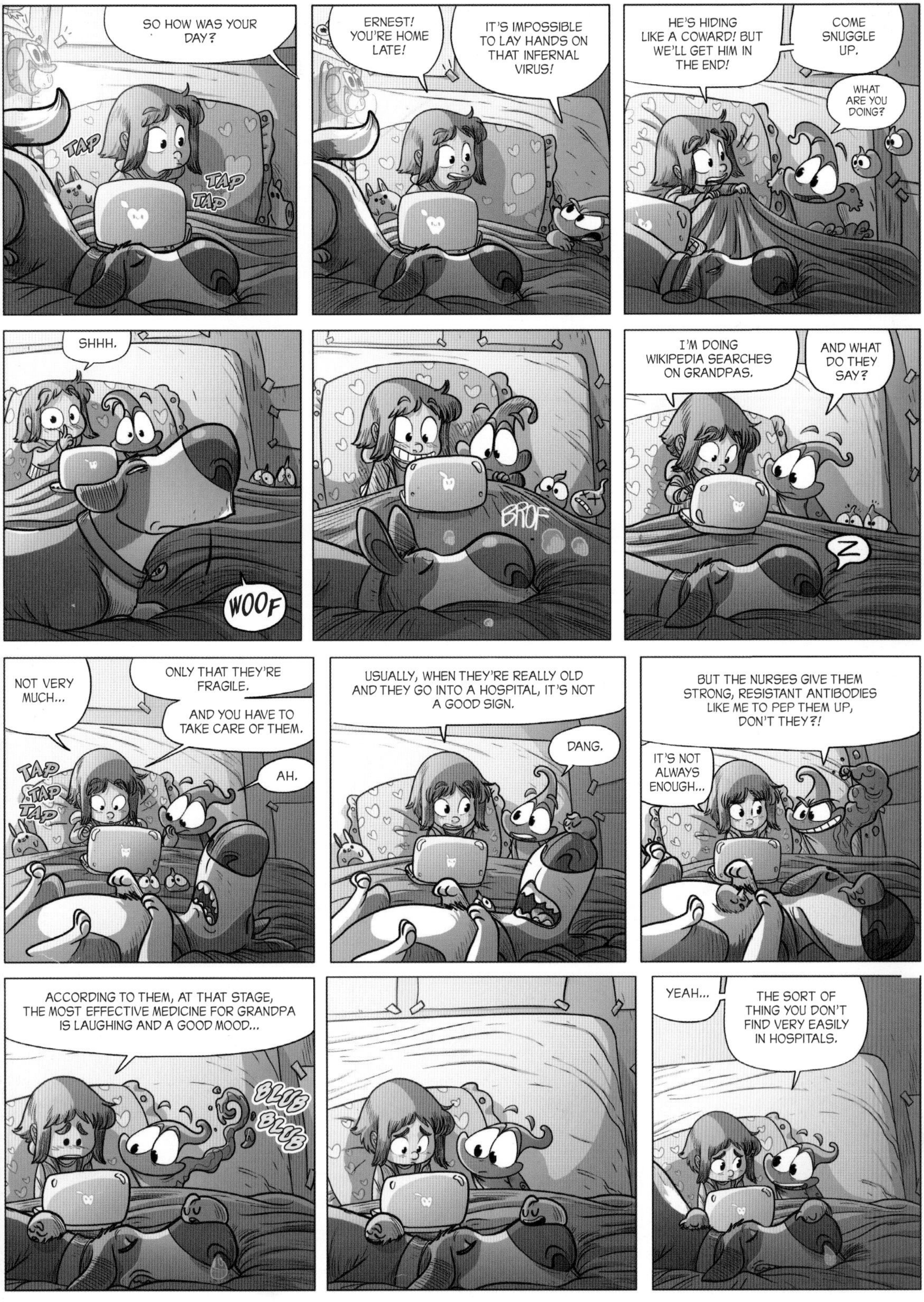
SO HOW WAS YOUR DAY?
TAP
TAP
TAP
ERNEST! YOU'RE HOME LATE!
IT'S IMPOSSIBLE TO LAY HANDS ON THAT INFERNAL VIRUS!
HE'S HIDING LIKE A COWARD! BUT WE'LL GET HIM IN THE END!
COME SNUGGLE UP.
WHAT ARE YOU DOING?
SHHH.
WOOF
BROF
I'M DOING WIKIPEDIA SEARCHES ON GRANDPAS.
AND WHAT DO THEY SAY?
Z
NOT VERY MUCH...
ONLY THAT THEY'RE FRAGILE.
AND YOU HAVE TO TAKE CARE OF THEM.
AH.
TAP
TAP
TAP
USUALLY, WHEN THEY'RE REALLY OLD AND THEY GO INTO A HOSPITAL, IT'S NOT A GOOD SIGN.
DANG.
BUT THE NURSES GIVE THEM STRONG, RESISTANT ANTIBODIES LIKE ME TO PEP THEM UP, DON'T THEY?!
IT'S NOT ALWAYS ENOUGH...
ACCORDING TO THEM, AT THAT STAGE, THE MOST EFFECTIVE MEDICINE FOR GRANDPA IS LAUGHING AND A GOOD MOOD...
BLUB
BLUB
YEAH...
THE SORT OF THING YOU DON'T FIND VERY EASILY IN HOSPITALS.

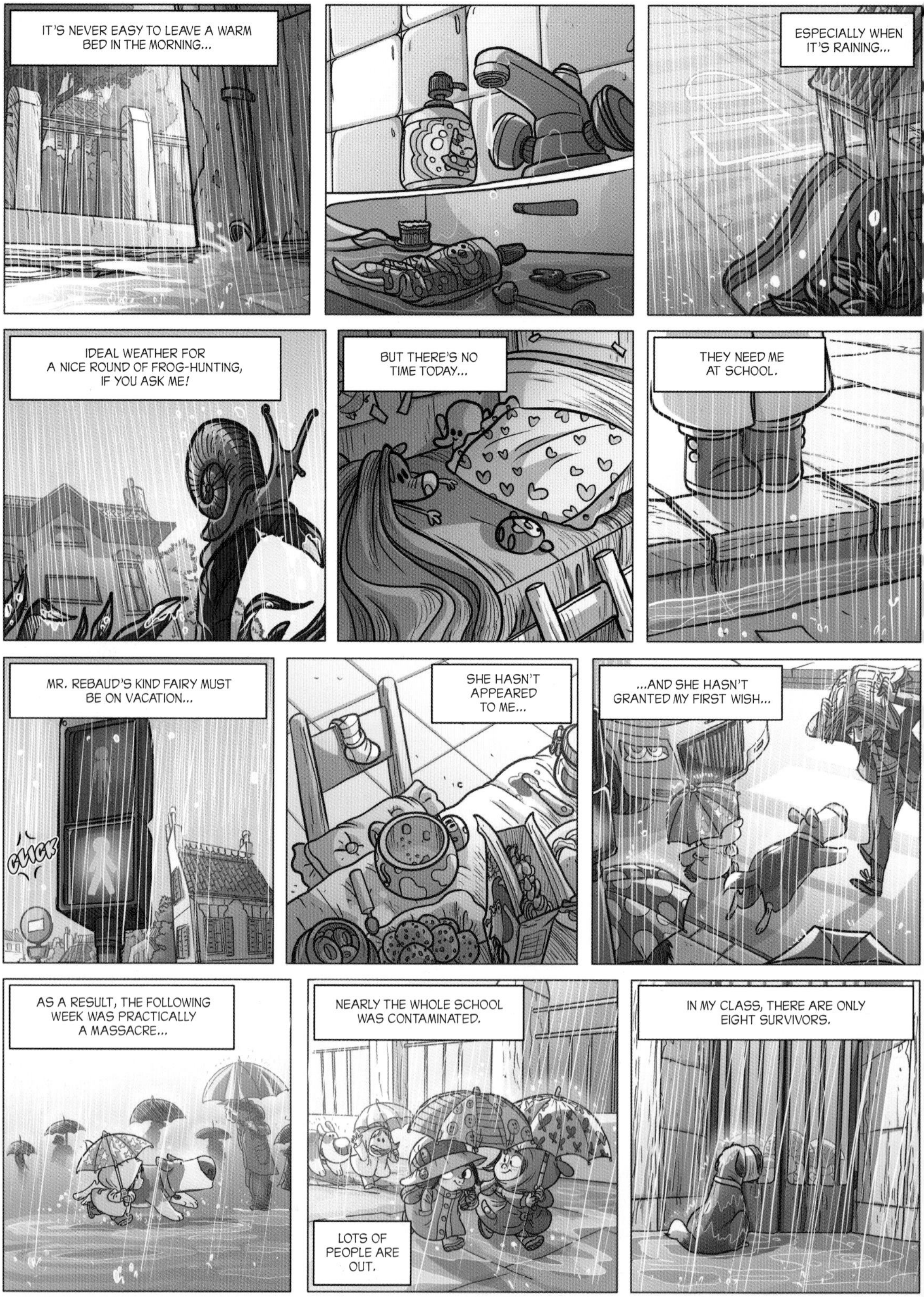
IT'S NEVER EASY TO LEAVE A WARM BED IN THE MORNING...
ESPECIALLY WHEN IT'S RAINING...
IDEAL WEATHER FOR A NICE ROUND OF FROG-HUNTING, IF YOU ASK ME!
BUT THERE'S NO TIME TODAY...
THEY NEED ME AT SCHOOL.
MR. REBAUD'S KIND FAIRY MUST BE ON VACATION...
CLICK
SHE HASN'T APPEARED TO ME...
...AND SHE HASN'T GRANTED MY FIRST WISH...
AS A RESULT, THE FOLLOWING WEEK WAS PRACTICALLY A MASSACRE...
NEARLY THE WHOLE SCHOOL WAS CONTAMINATED.
LOTS OF PEOPLE ARE OUT.
IN MY CLASS, THERE ARE ONLY EIGHT SURVIVORS.

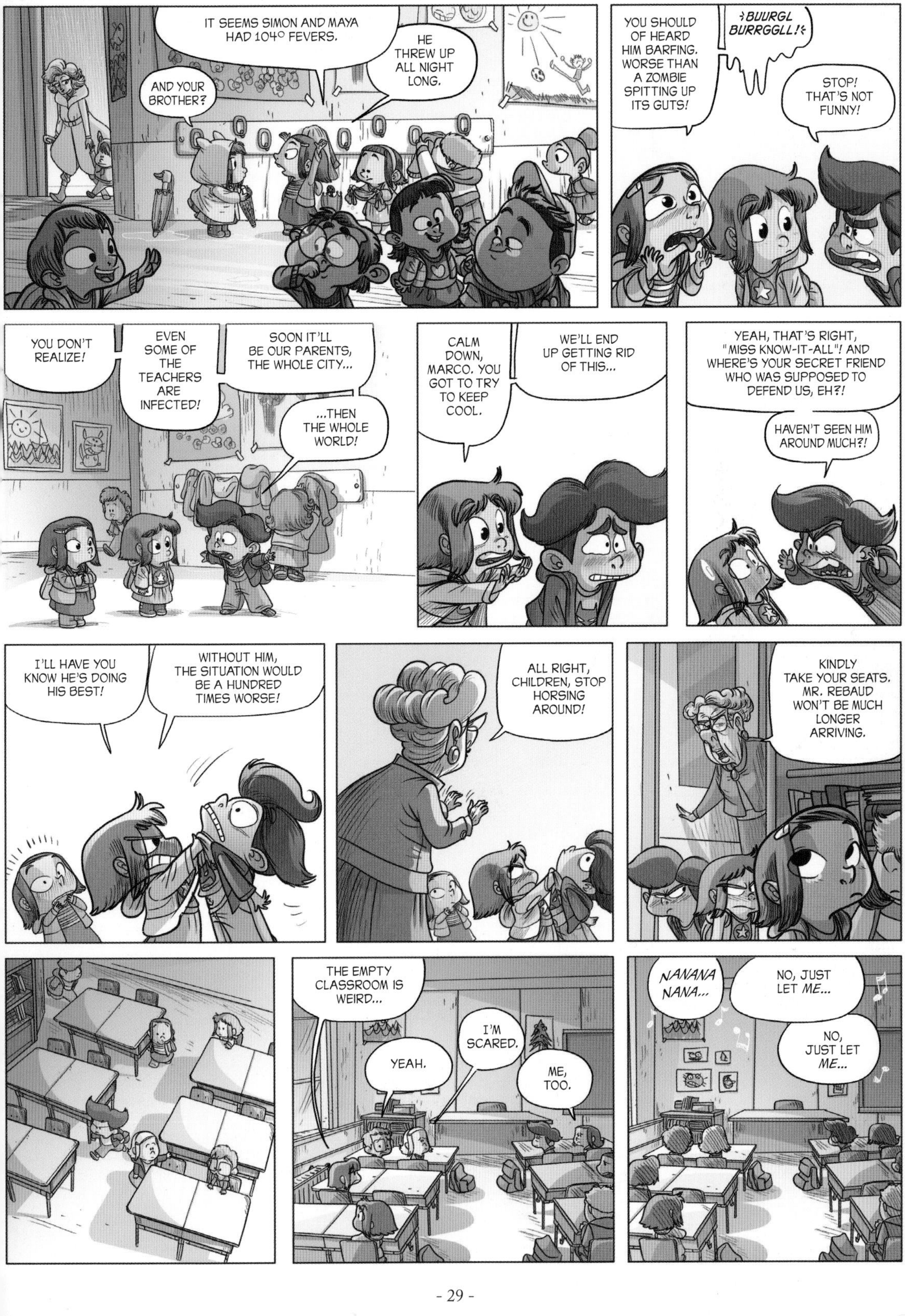
IT SEEMS SIMON AND MAYA HAD 104° FEVERS.
AND YOUR BROTHER?
HE THREW UP ALL NIGHT LONG.
YOU SHOULD OF HEARD HIM BARFING. WORSE THAN A ZOMBIE SPITTING UP ITS GUTS!
BUURGL BURRGGLL!
STOP! THAT'S NOT FUNNY!
YOU DON'T REALIZE!
EVEN SOME OF THE TEACHERS ARE INFECTED!
SOON IT'LL BE OUR PARENTS, THE WHOLE CITY...
...THEN THE WHOLE WORLD!
CALM DOWN, MARCO. YOU GOT TO TRY TO KEEP COOL.
WE'LL END UP GETTING RID OF THIS...
YEAH, THAT'S RIGHT, "MISS KNOW-IT-ALL"! AND WHERE'S YOUR SECRET FRIEND WHO WAS SUPPOSED TO DEFEND US, EH?!
HAVEN'T SEEN HIM AROUND MUCH?!
I'LL HAVE YOU KNOW HE'S DOING HIS BEST!
WITHOUT HIM, THE SITUATION WOULD BE A HUNDRED TIMES WORSE!
ALL RIGHT, CHILDREN, STOP HORSING AROUND!
KINDLY TAKE YOUR SEATS. MR. REBAUD WON'T BE MUCH LONGER ARRIVING.
THE EMPTY CLASSROOM IS WEIRD...
YEAH.
I'M SCARED.
ME, TOO.
NANANA NANA...
NO, JUST LET ME...
NO, JUST LET ME...

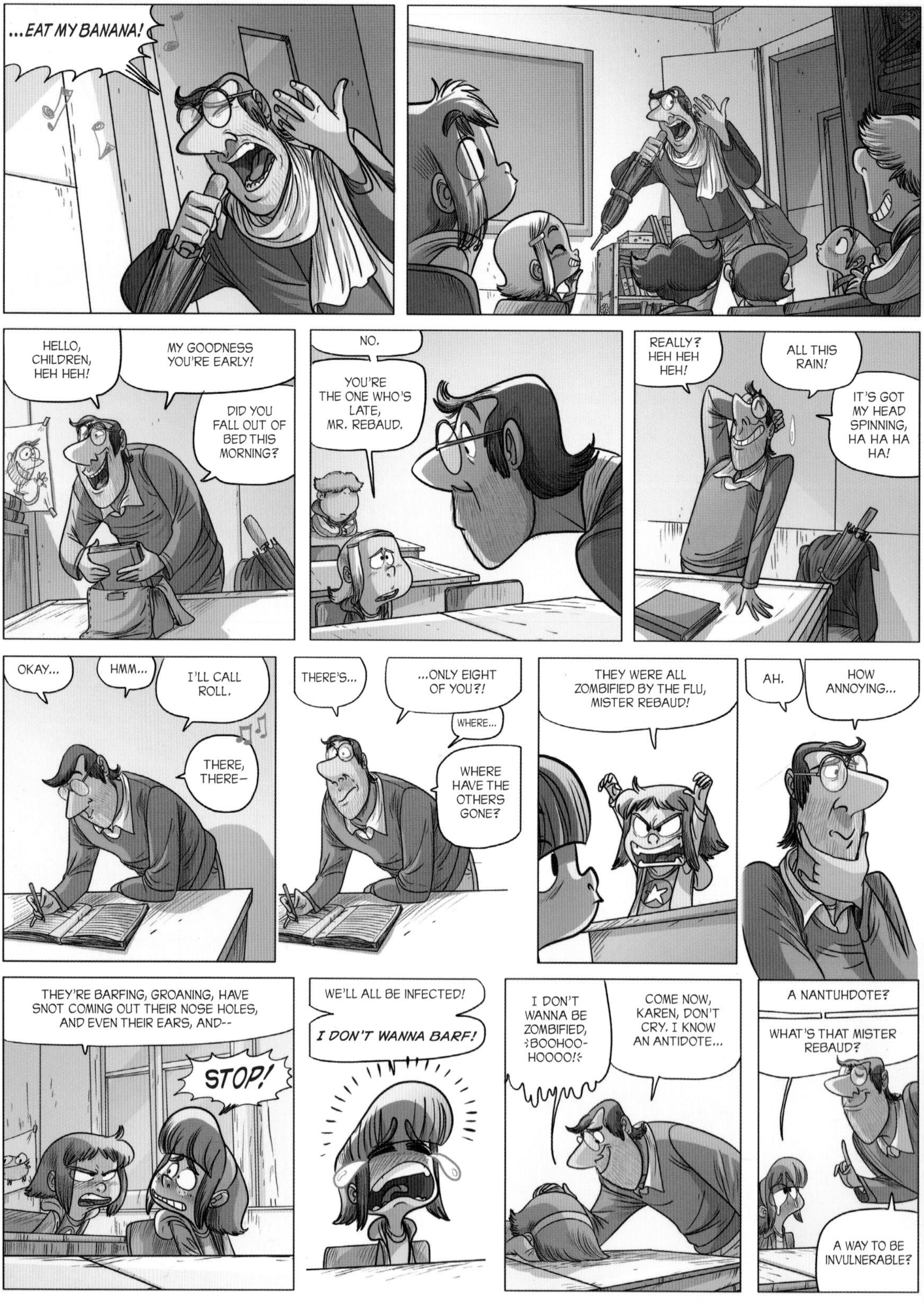
...EAT MY BANANA!
HELLO, CHILDREN, HEH HEH!
MY GOODNESS YOU'RE EARLY!
DID YOU FALL OUT OF BED THIS MORNING?
NO.
YOU'RE THE ONE WHO'S LATE, MR. REBAUD.
REALLY? HEH HEH HEH!
ALL THIS RAIN!
IT'S GOT MY HEAD SPINNING, HA HA HA HA!
OKAY...
HMM...
I'LL CALL ROLL.
THERE, THERE–
THERE'S...
...ONLY EIGHT OF YOU?!
WHERE...
WHERE HAVE THE OTHERS GONE?
THEY WERE ALL ZOMBIFIED BY THE FLU, MISTER REBAUD!
AH.
HOW ANNOYING...
THEY'RE BARFING, GROANING, HAVE SNOT COMING OUT THEIR NOSE HOLES, AND EVEN THEIR EARS, AND--
STOP!
WE'LL ALL BE INFECTED!
I DON'T WANNA BARF!
I DON'T WANNA BE ZOMBIFIED, BOOHOO-HOOOO!
COME NOW, KAREN, DON'T CRY. I KNOW AN ANTIDOTE...
A NANTUHDOTE?
WHAT'S THAT MISTER REBAUD?
A WAY TO BE INVULNERABLE?

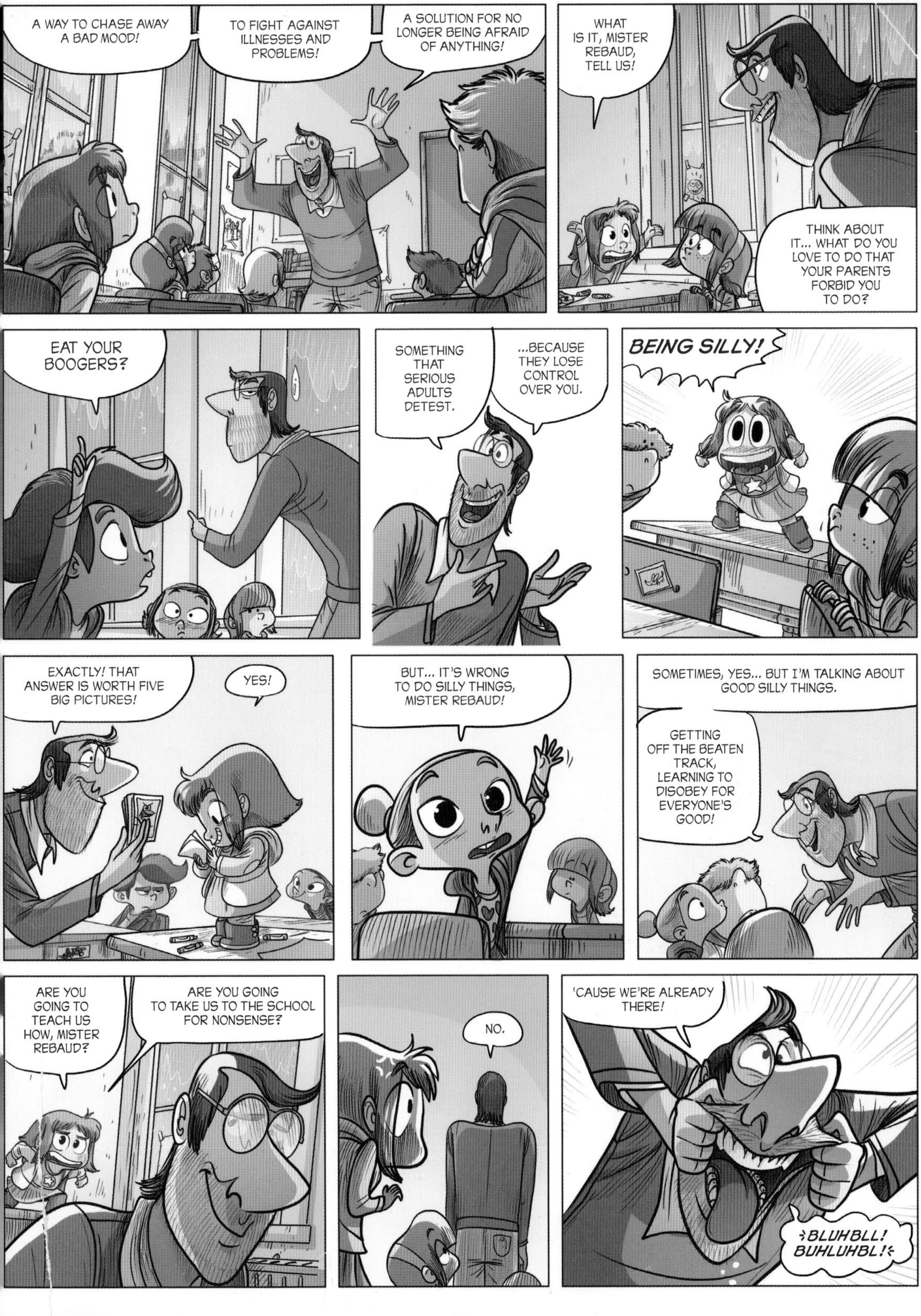
A WAY TO CHASE AWAY A BAD MOOD!
TO FIGHT AGAINST ILLNESSES AND PROBLEMS!
A SOLUTION FOR NO LONGER BEING AFRAID OF ANYTHING!
WHAT IS IT, MISTER REBAUD, TELL US!
THINK ABOUT IT... WHAT DO YOU LOVE TO DO THAT YOUR PARENTS FORBID YOU TO DO?
EAT YOUR BOOGERS?
SOMETHING THAT SERIOUS ADULTS DETEST.
...BECAUSE THEY LOSE CONTROL OVER YOU.
BEING SILLY!
EXACTLY! THAT ANSWER IS WORTH FIVE BIG PICTURES!
YES!
BUT... IT'S WRONG TO DO SILLY THINGS, MISTER REBAUD!
SOMETIMES, YES... BUT I'M TALKING ABOUT GOOD SILLY THINGS.
GETTING OFF THE BEATEN TRACK, LEARNING TO DISOBEY FOR EVERYONE'S GOOD!
ARE YOU GOING TO TEACH US HOW, MISTER REBAUD?
ARE YOU GOING TO TAKE US TO THE SCHOOL FOR NONSENSE?
NO.
'CAUSE WE'RE ALREADY THERE!
BLUHBLL! BUHLUHBL!

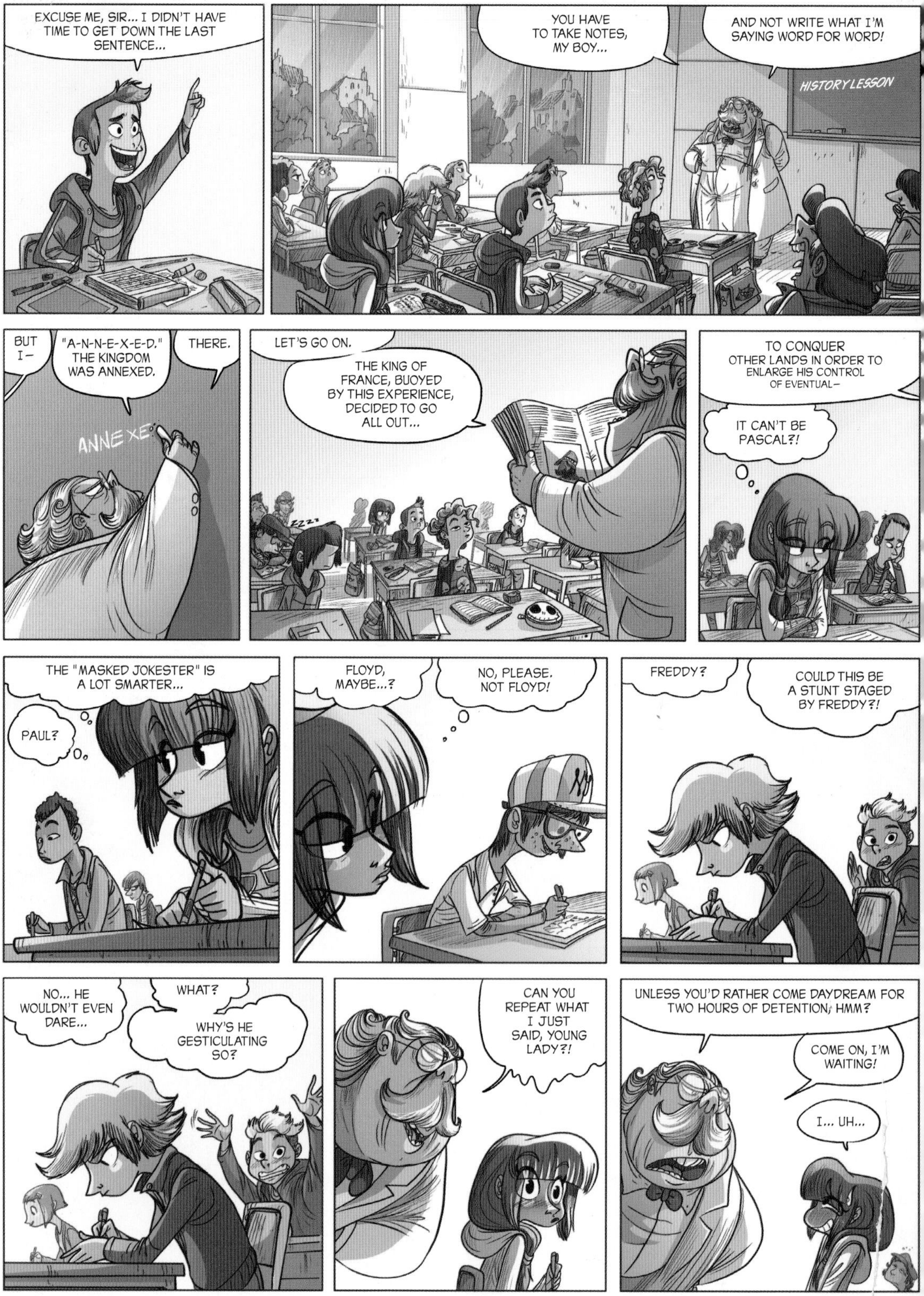
EXCUSE ME, SIR... I DIDN'T HAVE TIME TO GET DOWN THE LAST SENTENCE...
YOU HAVE TO TAKE NOTES, MY BOY...
AND NOT WRITE WHAT I'M SAYING WORD FOR WORD!
HISTORY LESSON
BUT I—
"A-N-N-E-X-E-D." THE KINGDOM WAS ANNEXED.
THERE.
ANNEXE:
LET'S GO ON.
THE KING OF FRANCE, BUOYED BY THIS EXPERIENCE, DECIDED TO GO ALL OUT...
TO CONQUER OTHER LANDS IN ORDER TO ENLARGE HIS CONTROL OF EVENTUAL—
IT CAN'T BE PASCAL?!
THE "MASKED JOKESTER" IS A LOT SMARTER...
PAUL?
FLOYD, MAYBE...?
NO, PLEASE. NOT FLOYD!
FREDDY?
COULD THIS BE A STUNT STAGED BY FREDDY?!
NO... HE WOULDN'T EVEN DARE...
WHAT?
WHY'S HE GESTICULATING SO?
CAN YOU REPEAT WHAT I JUST SAID, YOUNG LADY?!
UNLESS YOU'D RATHER COME DAYDREAM FOR TWO HOURS OF DETENTION, HMM?
COME ON, I'M WAITING!
I... UH...

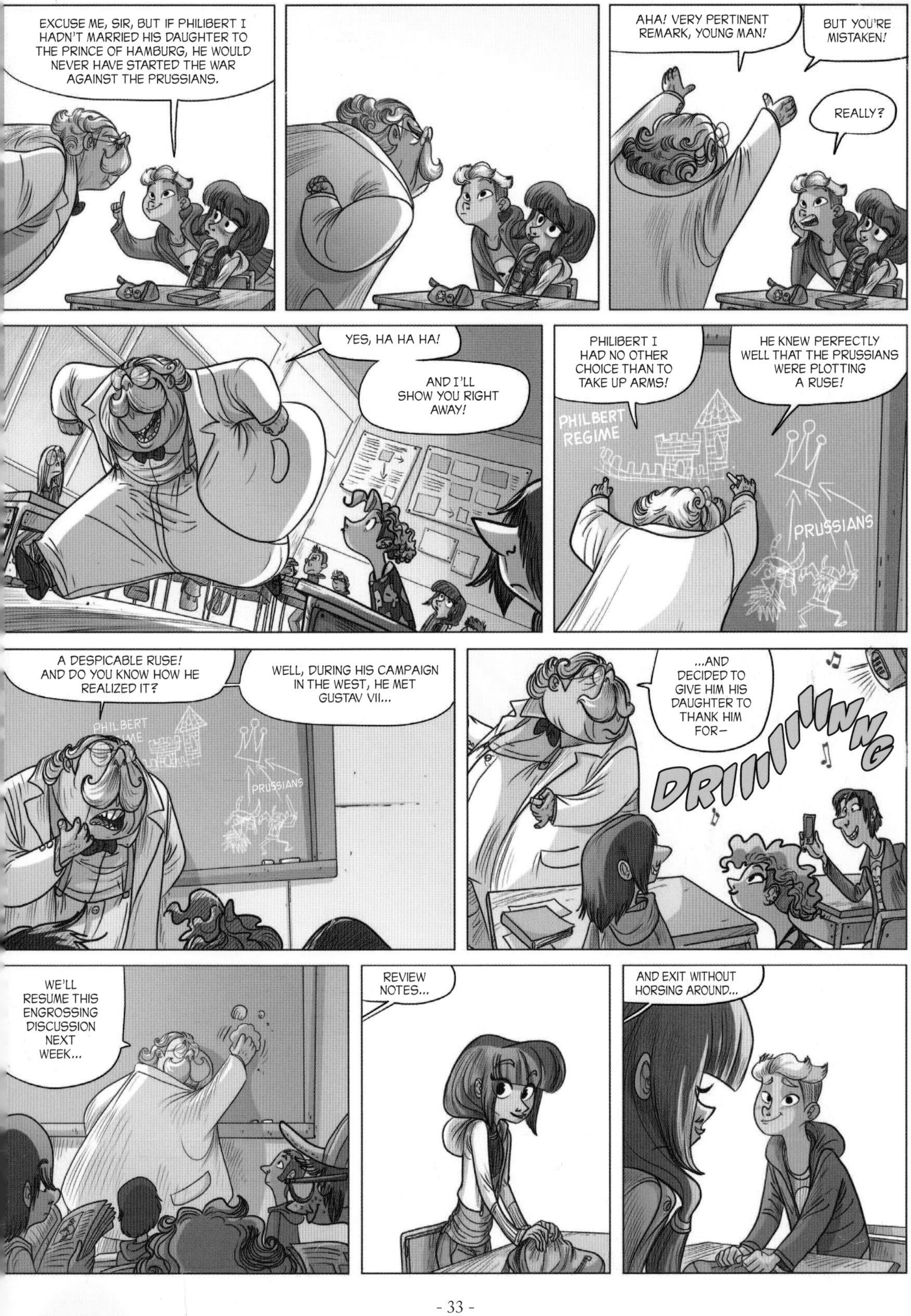
EXCUSE ME, SIR, BUT IF PHILIBERT I HADN'T MARRIED HIS DAUGHTER TO THE PRINCE OF HAMBURG, HE WOULD NEVER HAVE STARTED THE WAR AGAINST THE PRUSSIANS.
AHA! VERY PERTINENT REMARK, YOUNG MAN!
BUT YOU'RE MISTAKEN!
REALLY?
YES, HA HA HA!
AND I'LL SHOW YOU RIGHT AWAY!
PHILIBERT I HAD NO OTHER CHOICE THAN TO TAKE UP ARMS!
HE KNEW PERFECTLY WELL THAT THE PRUSSIANS WERE PLOTTING A RUSE!
PHILBERT REGIME
PRUSSIANS
A DESPICABLE RUSE! AND DO YOU KNOW HOW HE REALIZED IT?
WELL, DURING HIS CAMPAIGN IN THE WEST, HE MET GUSTAV VII...
...AND DECIDED TO GIVE HIM HIS DAUGHTER TO THANK HIM FOR–
DRIIIIIIINNG
WE'LL RESUME THIS ENGROSSING DISCUSSION NEXT WEEK...
REVIEW NOTES...
AND EXIT WITHOUT HORSING AROUND...

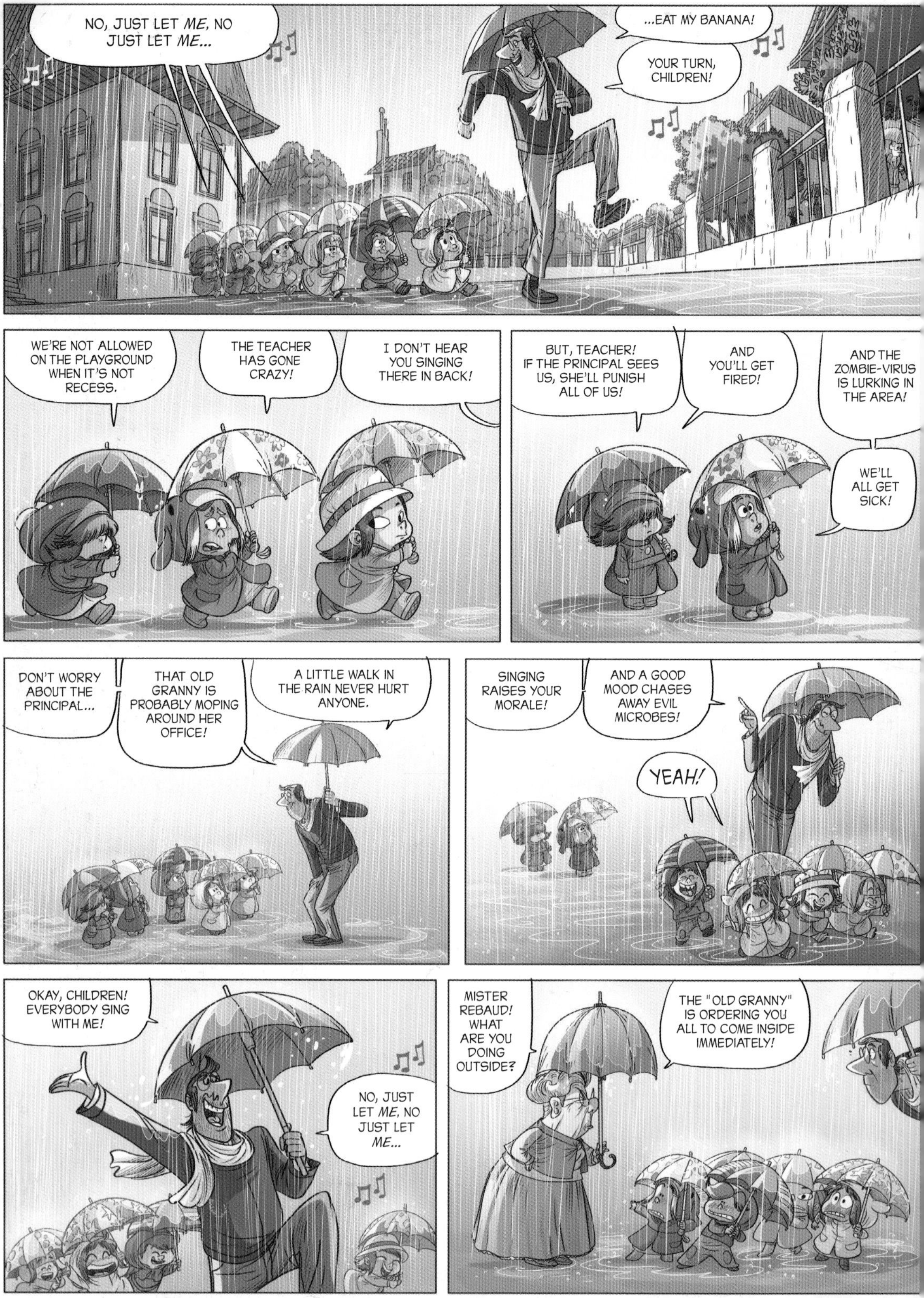
NO, JUST LET ME, NO JUST LET ME...
...EAT MY BANANA!
YOUR TURN, CHILDREN!
WE'RE NOT ALLOWED ON THE PLAYGROUND WHEN IT'S NOT RECESS.
THE TEACHER HAS GONE CRAZY!
I DON'T HEAR YOU SINGING THERE IN BACK!
BUT, TEACHER! IF THE PRINCIPAL SEES US, SHE'LL PUNISH ALL OF US!
AND YOU'LL GET FIRED!
AND THE ZOMBIE-VIRUS IS LURKING IN THE AREA!
WE'LL ALL GET SICK!
DON'T WORRY ABOUT THE PRINCIPAL...
THAT OLD GRANNY IS PROBABLY MOPING AROUND HER OFFICE!
A LITTLE WALK IN THE RAIN NEVER HURT ANYONE.
SINGING RAISES YOUR MORALE!
AND A GOOD MOOD CHASES AWAY EVIL MICROBES!
YEAH!
OKAY, CHILDREN! EVERYBODY SING WITH ME!
NO, JUST LET ME, NO JUST LET ME...
MISTER REBAUD! WHAT ARE YOU DOING OUTSIDE?
THE "OLD GRANNY" IS ORDERING YOU ALL TO COME INSIDE IMMEDIATELY!

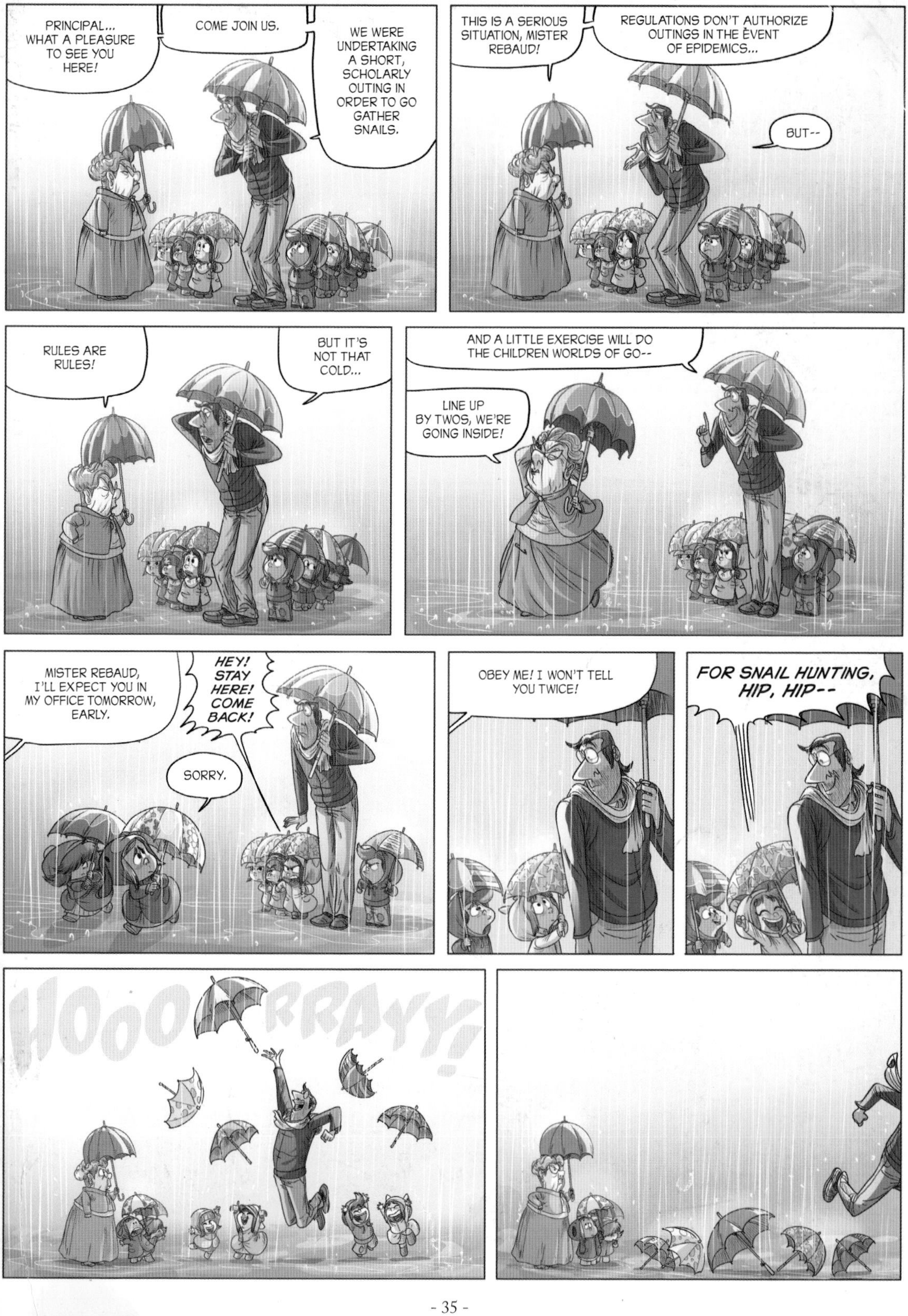
PRINCIPAL... WHAT A PLEASURE TO SEE YOU HERE!
COME JOIN US.
WE WERE UNDERTAKING A SHORT, SCHOLARLY OUTING IN ORDER TO GO GATHER SNAILS.
THIS IS A SERIOUS SITUATION, MISTER REBAUD!
REGULATIONS DON'T AUTHORIZE OUTINGS IN THE EVENT OF EPIDEMICS...
BUT--
RULES ARE RULES!
BUT IT'S NOT THAT COLD...
AND A LITTLE EXERCISE WILL DO THE CHILDREN WORLDS OF GO--
LINE UP BY TWOS, WE'RE GOING INSIDE!
MISTER REBAUD, I'LL EXPECT YOU IN MY OFFICE TOMORROW, EARLY.
HEY! STAY HERE! COME BACK!
SORRY.
OBEY ME! I WON'T TELL YOU TWICE!
FOR SNAIL HUNTING, HIP, HIP--
HOOOORRAYY!

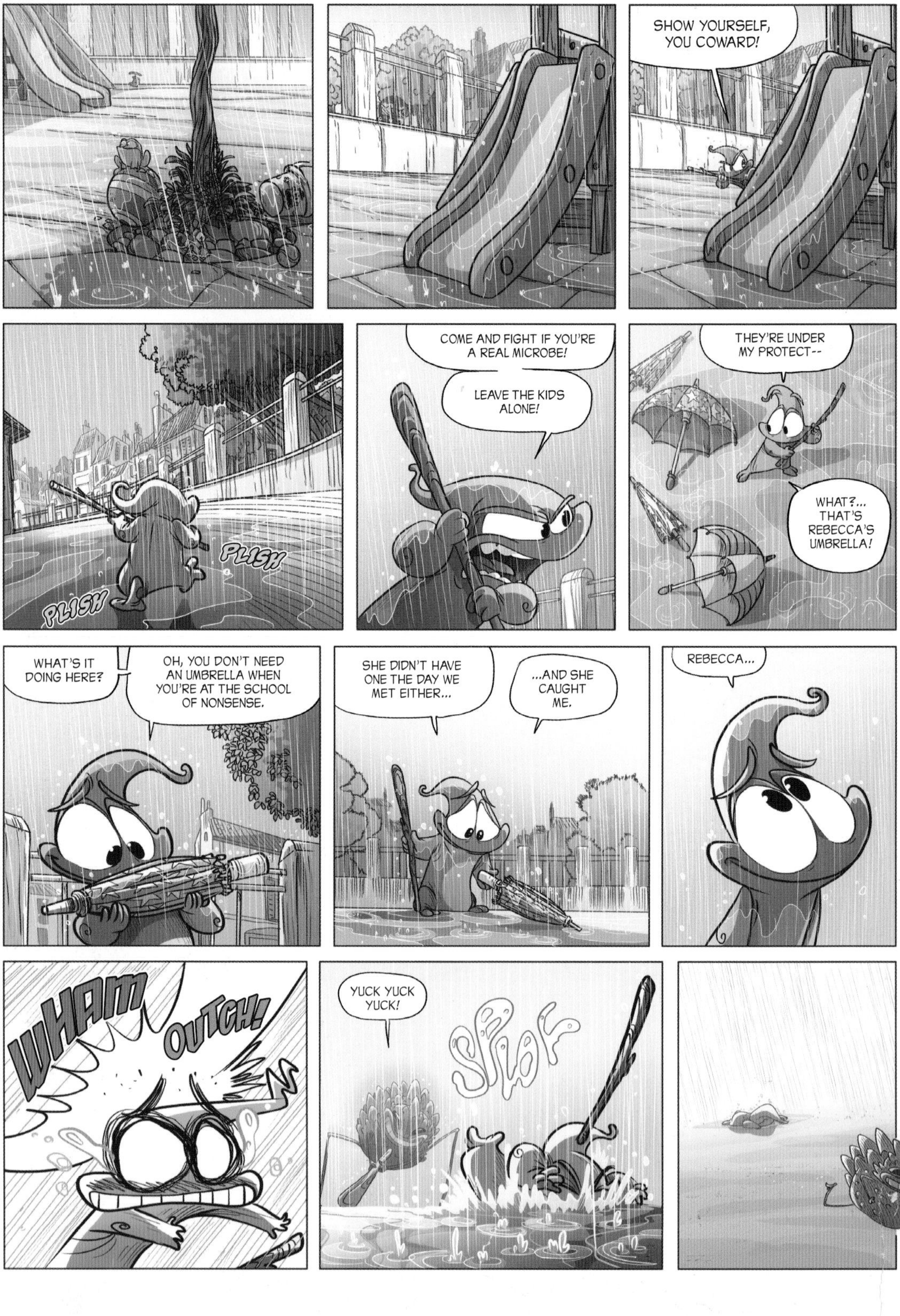
SHOW YOURSELF, YOU COWARD!
PLISH
PLISH
COME AND FIGHT IF YOU'RE A REAL MICROBE!
LEAVE THE KIDS ALONE!
THEY'RE UNDER MY PROTECT--
WHAT?... THAT'S REBECCA'S UMBRELLA!
WHAT'S IT DOING HERE?
OH, YOU DON'T NEED AN UMBRELLA WHEN YOU'RE AT THE SCHOOL OF NONSENSE.
SHE DIDN'T HAVE ONE THE DAY WE MET EITHER...
...AND SHE CAUGHT ME.
REBECCA...
WHAM
OUTCH!
YUCK YUCK YUCK!
SPLOF

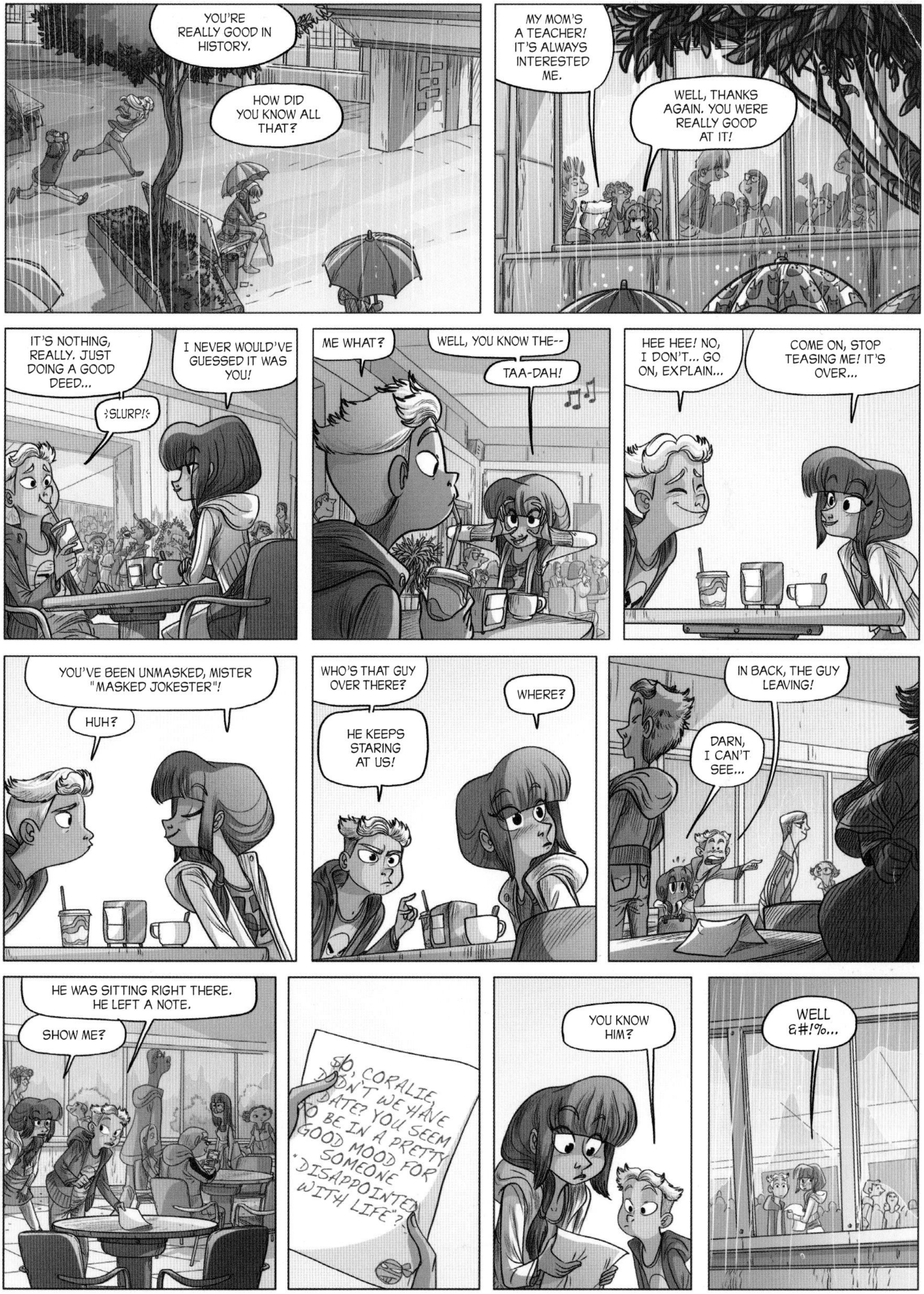
YOU'RE REALLY GOOD IN HISTORY.
HOW DID YOU KNOW ALL THAT?
MY MOM'S A TEACHER! IT'S ALWAYS INTERESTED ME.
WELL, THANKS AGAIN. YOU WERE REALLY GOOD AT IT!
IT'S NOTHING, REALLY. JUST DOING A GOOD DEED...
SLURP!
I NEVER WOULD'VE GUESSED IT WAS YOU!
ME WHAT?
WELL, YOU KNOW THE--
TAA-DAH!
HEE HEE! NO, I DON'T... GO ON, EXPLAIN...
COME ON, STOP TEASING ME! IT'S OVER...
YOU'VE BEEN UNMASKED, MISTER "MASKED JOKESTER"!
HUH?
WHO'S THAT GUY OVER THERE?
HE KEEPS STARING AT US!
WHERE?
IN BACK, THE GUY LEAVING!
DARN, I CAN'T SEE...
HE WAS SITTING RIGHT THERE. HE LEFT A NOTE.
SHOW ME?
SO, CORALIE, DIDN'T WE HAVE A DATE? YOU SEEM TO BE IN A PRETTY GOOD MOOD FOR SOMEONE "DISAPPOINTED WITH LIFE"?
YOU KNOW HIM?
WELL &#!%...

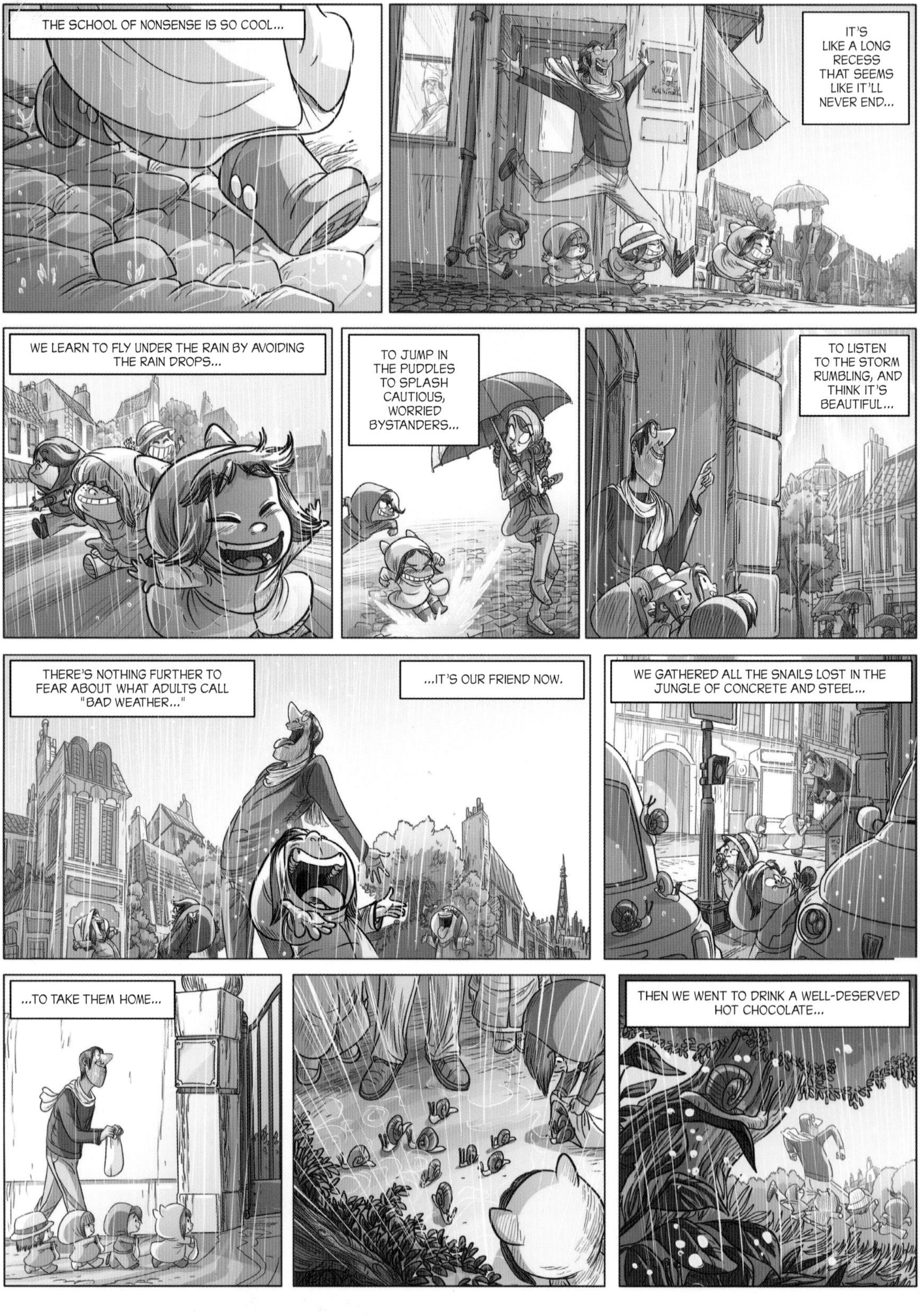
THE SCHOOL OF NONSENSE IS SO COOL...
IT'S LIKE A LONG RECESS THAT SEEMS LIKE IT'LL NEVER END...
WE LEARN TO FLY UNDER THE RAIN BY AVOIDING THE RAIN DROPS...
TO JUMP IN THE PUDDLES TO SPLASH CAUTIOUS, WORRIED BYSTANDERS...
TO LISTEN TO THE STORM RUMBLING, AND THINK IT'S BEAUTIFUL...
THERE'S NOTHING FURTHER TO FEAR ABOUT WHAT ADULTS CALL "BAD WEATHER..."
...IT'S OUR FRIEND NOW.
WE GATHERED ALL THE SNAILS LOST IN THE JUNGLE OF CONCRETE AND STEEL...
...TO TAKE THEM HOME...
THEN WE WENT TO DRINK A WELL-DESERVED HOT CHOCOLATE...

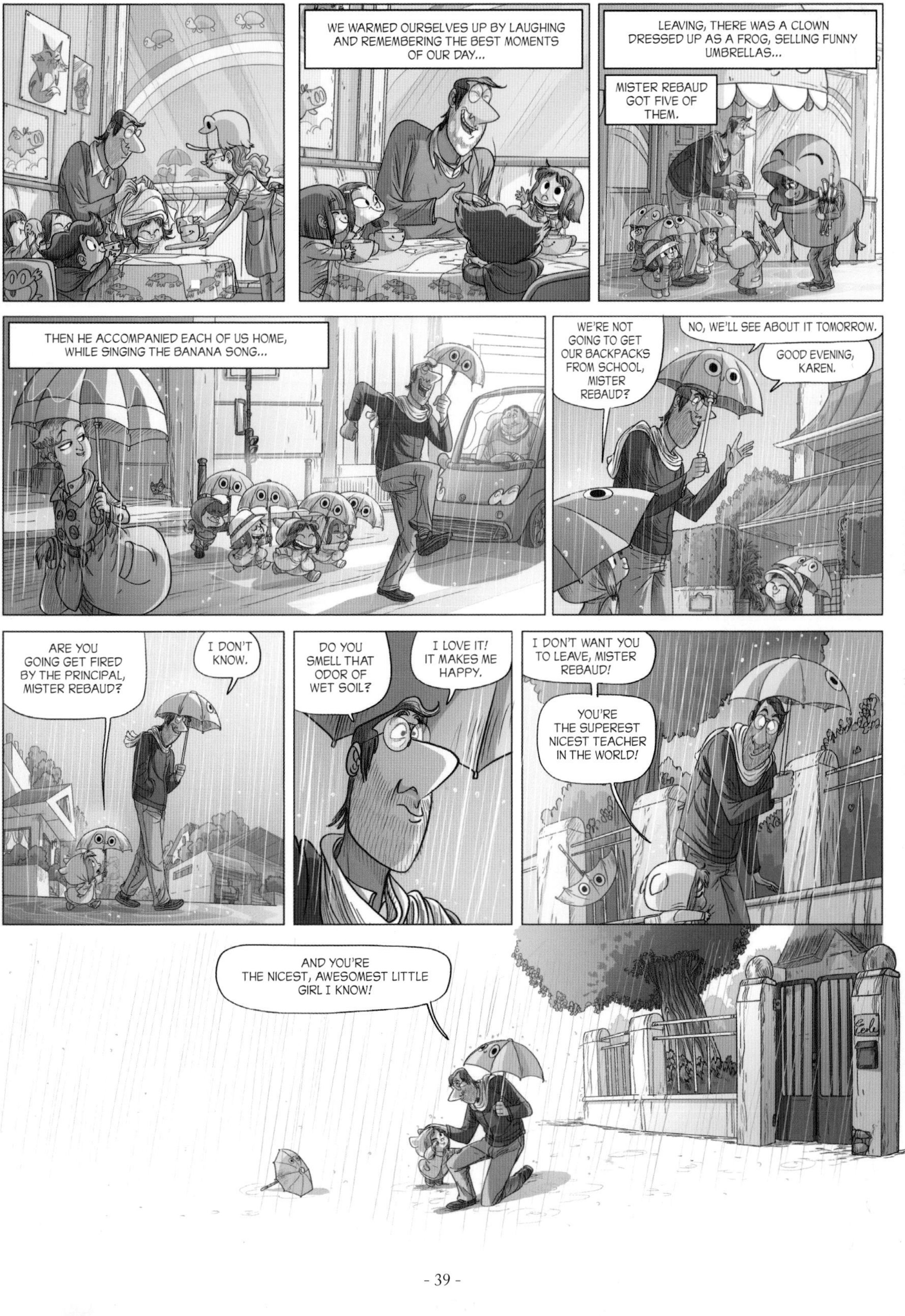
WE WARMED OURSELVES UP BY LAUGHING AND REMEMBERING THE BEST MOMENTS OF OUR DAY...
LEAVING, THERE WAS A CLOWN DRESSED UP AS A FROG, SELLING FUNNY UMBRELLAS...
MISTER REBAUD GOT FIVE OF THEM.
THEN HE ACCOMPANIED EACH OF US HOME, WHILE SINGING THE BANANA SONG...
WE'RE NOT GOING TO GET OUR BACKPACKS FROM SCHOOL, MISTER REBAUD?
NO, WE'LL SEE ABOUT IT TOMORROW.
GOOD EVENING, KAREN.
ARE YOU GOING GET FIRED BY THE PRINCIPAL, MISTER REBAUD?
I DON'T KNOW.
DO YOU SMELL THAT ODOR OF WET SOIL?
I LOVE IT! IT MAKES ME HAPPY.
I DON'T WANT YOU TO LEAVE, MISTER REBAUD!
YOU'RE THE SUPEREST NICEST TEACHER IN THE WORLD!
AND YOU'RE THE NICEST, AWESOMEST LITTLE GIRL I KNOW!

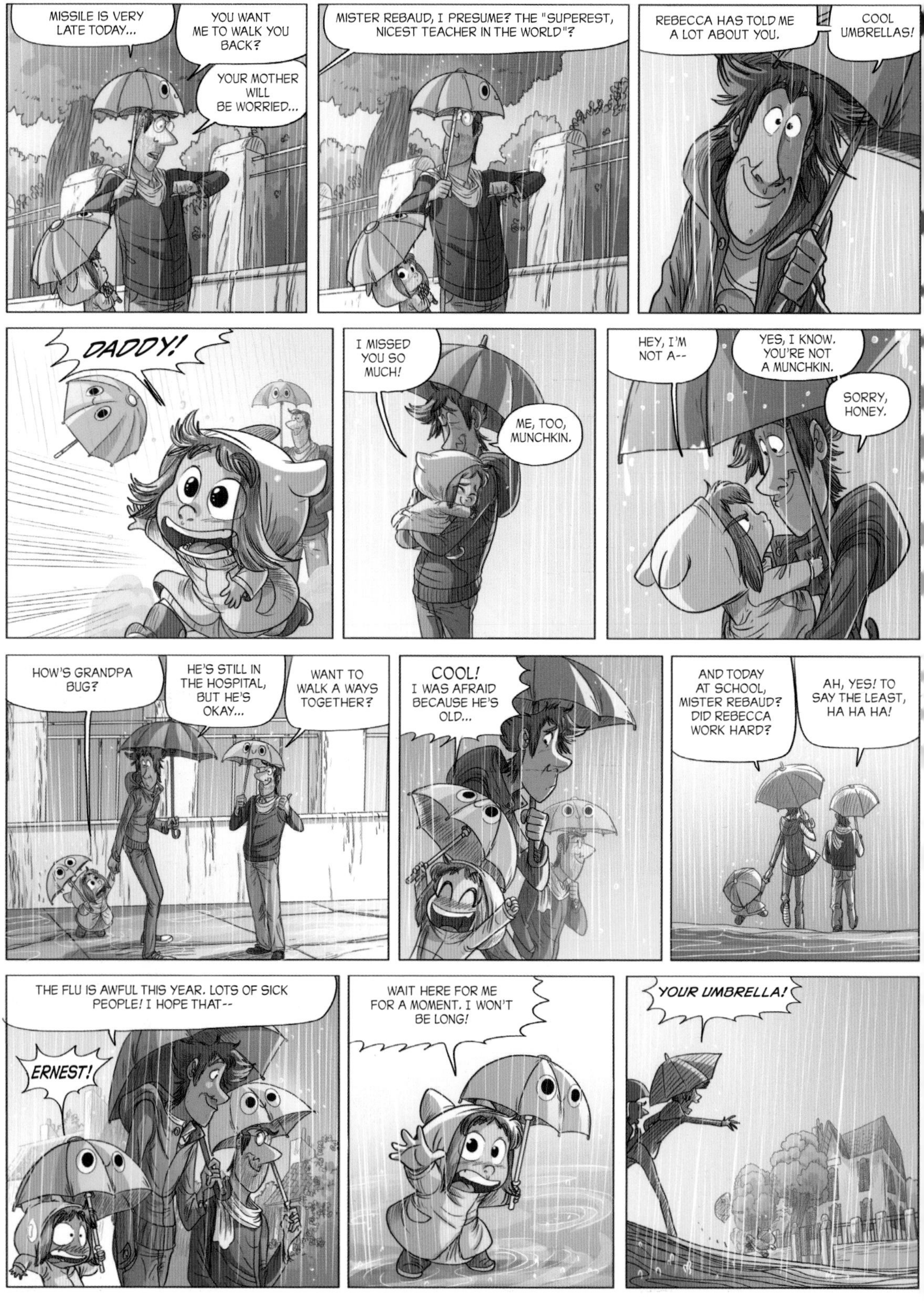
MISSILE IS VERY LATE TODAY...
YOU WANT ME TO WALK YOU BACK?
YOUR MOTHER WILL BE WORRIED...
MISTER REBAUD, I PRESUME? THE "SUPEREST, NICEST TEACHER IN THE WORLD"?
REBECCA HAS TOLD ME A LOT ABOUT YOU.
COOL UMBRELLAS!
DADDY!
I MISSED YOU SO MUCH!
ME, TOO, MUNCHKIN.
HEY, I'M NOT A--
YES, I KNOW. YOU'RE NOT A MUNCHKIN.
SORRY, HONEY.
HOW'S GRANDPA BUG?
HE'S STILL IN THE HOSPITAL, BUT HE'S OKAY...
WANT TO WALK A WAYS TOGETHER?
COOL! I WAS AFRAID BECAUSE HE'S OLD...
AND TODAY AT SCHOOL, MISTER REBAUD? DID REBECCA WORK HARD?
AH, YES! TO SAY THE LEAST, HA HA HA!
THE FLU IS AWFUL THIS YEAR. LOTS OF SICK PEOPLE! I HOPE THAT--
ERNEST!
WAIT HERE FOR ME FOR A MOMENT. I WON'T BE LONG!
YOUR UMBRELLA!

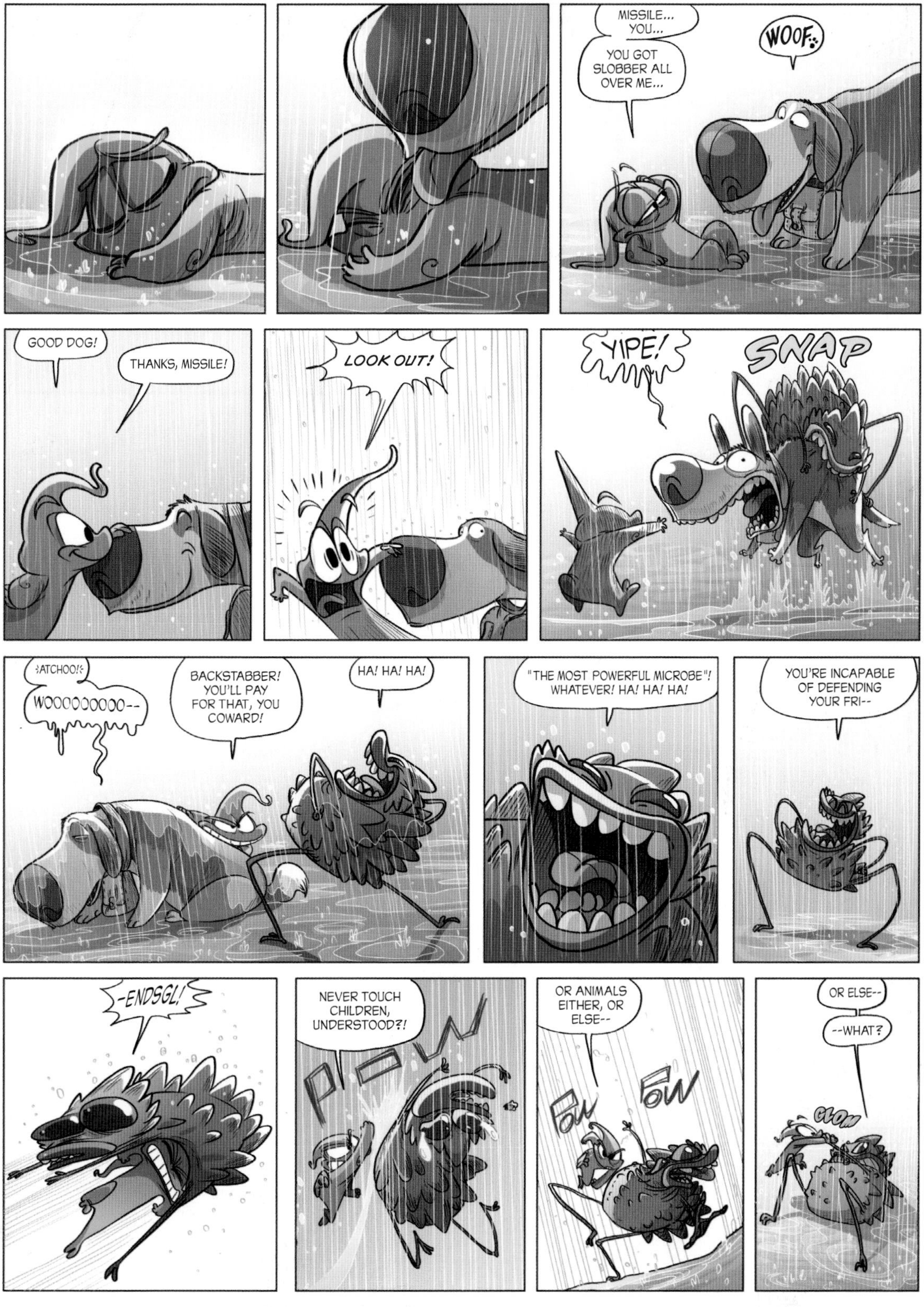
MISSILE... YOU...
YOU GOT SLOBBER ALL OVER ME...
WOOF
GOOD DOG!
THANKS, MISSILE!
LOOK OUT!
YIPE!
SNAP
ATCHOO!
WOOOOOOOOO--
BACKSTABBER! YOU'LL PAY FOR THAT, YOU COWARD!
HA! HA! HA!
"THE MOST POWERFUL MICROBE"! WHATEVER! HA! HA! HA!
YOU'RE INCAPABLE OF DEFENDING YOUR FRI--
-ENDSGL!
NEVER TOUCH CHILDREN, UNDERSTOOD?!
POW
OR ANIMALS EITHER, OR ELSE--
POW POW
OR ELSE--
--WHAT?
GLOM

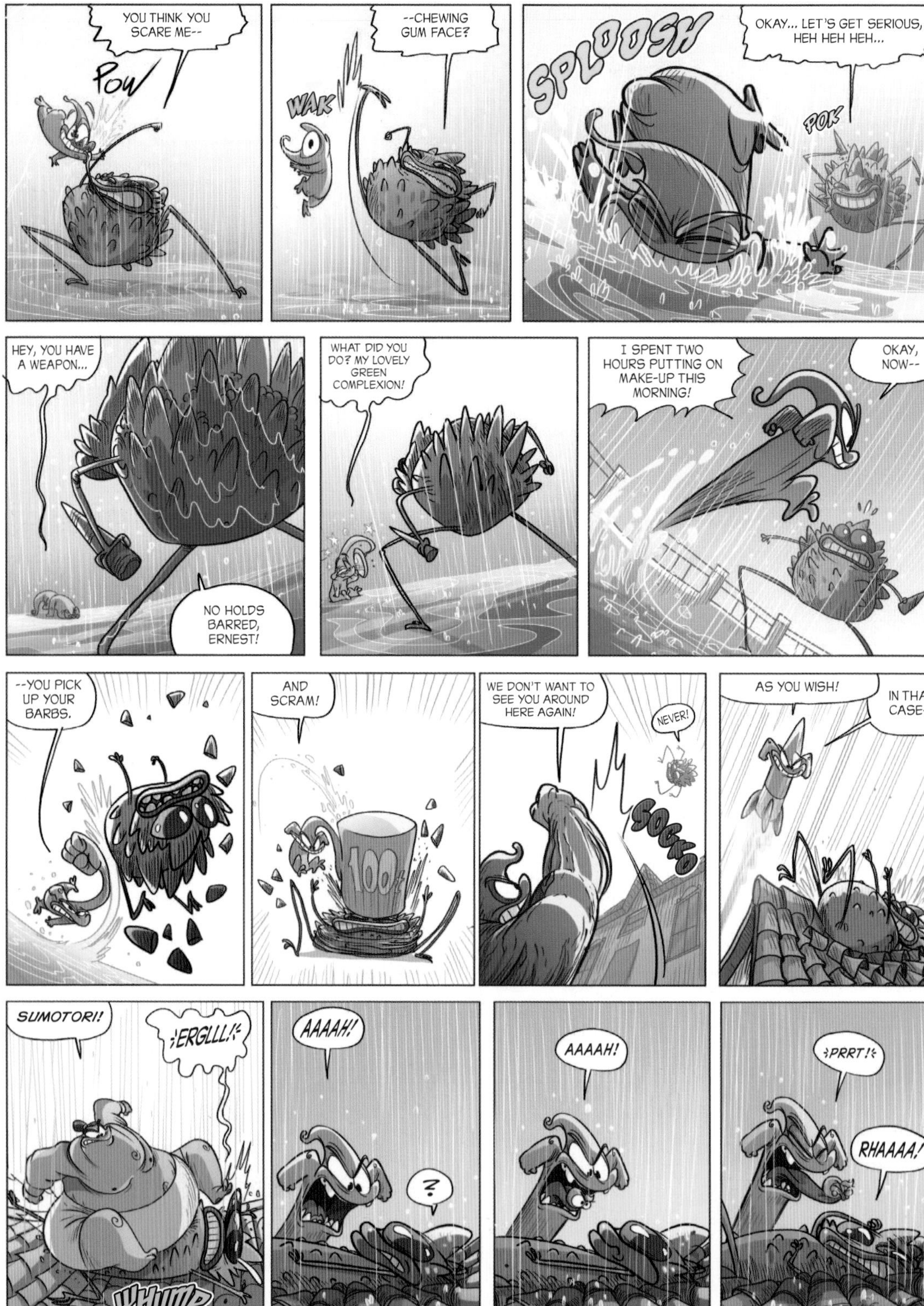
YOU THINK YOU SCARE ME--
POW
--CHEWING GUM FACE?
WAK
SPLOOSH
OKAY... LET'S GET SERIOUS, HEH HEH HEH...
POK
HEY, YOU HAVE A WEAPON...
NO HOLDS BARRED, ERNEST!
WHAT DID YOU DO? MY LOVELY GREEN COMPLEXION!
I SPENT TWO HOURS PUTTING ON MAKE-UP THIS MORNING!
OKAY, NOW--
--YOU PICK UP YOUR BARBS.
AND SCRAM!
100t
WE DON'T WANT TO SEE YOU AROUND HERE AGAIN!
NEVER!
SOCKO
AS YOU WISH!
IN THAT CASE--
SUMOTORI!
ERGLLL!
WHUMP
AAAAH!
?
AAAAH!
PRRT!
RHAAAA!

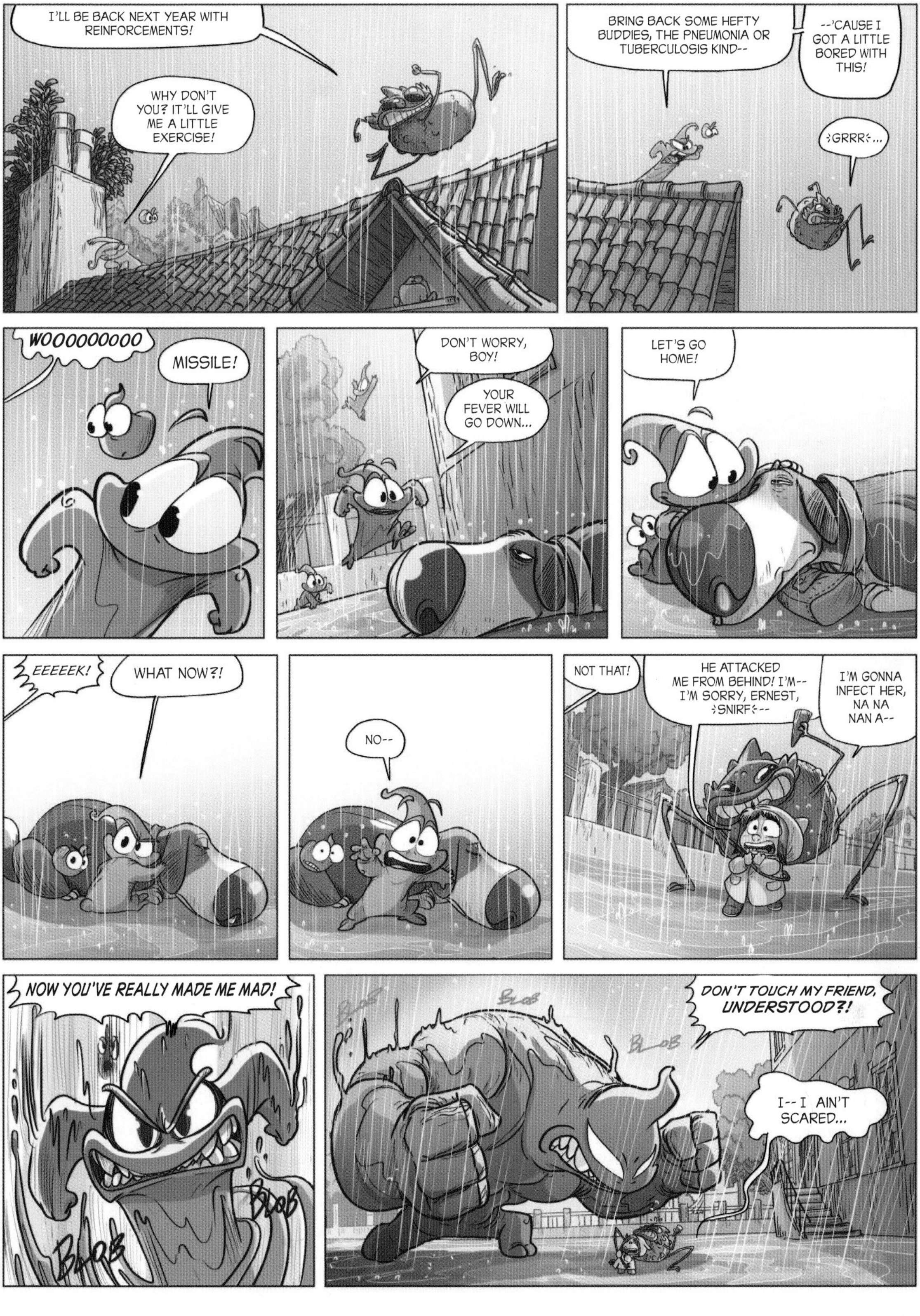

I'LL BE BACK NEXT YEAR WITH REINFORCEMENTS!
WHY DON'T YOU? IT'LL GIVE ME A LITTLE EXERCISE!
BRING BACK SOME HEFTY BUDDIES, THE PNEUMONIA OR TUBERCULOSIS KIND--
--'CAUSE I GOT A LITTLE BORED WITH THIS!
GRRR...
WOOOOOOOOO
MISSILE!
DON'T WORRY, BOY!
YOUR FEVER WILL GO DOWN...
LET'S GO HOME!
EEEEEK!
WHAT NOW?!
NO--
NOT THAT!
HE ATTACKED ME FROM BEHIND! I'M-- I'M SORRY, ERNEST, SNIRF--
I'M GONNA INFECT HER, NA NA NAN A--
NOW YOU'VE REALLY MADE ME MAD!
BLOB
BLOB
BLOB
BLOB
BLOB
DON'T TOUCH MY FRIEND, UNDERSTOOD?!
I-- I AIN'T SCARED...

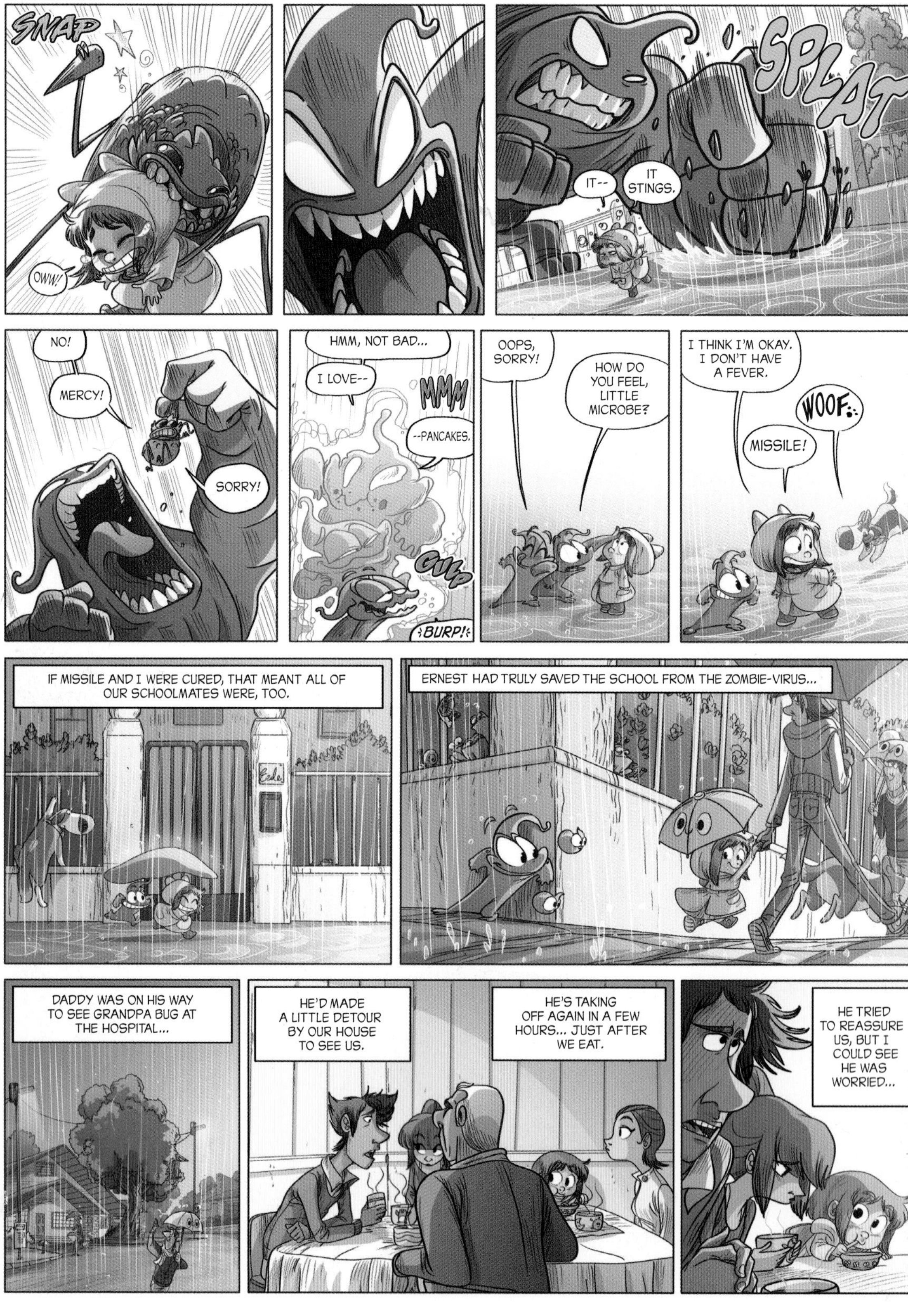

SNAP
OWW!
SPLAT
IT--
IT STINGS.
NO!
MERCY!
SORRY!
HMM, NOT BAD...
I LOVE--
MMM
--PANCAKES.
GULP
BURP!
OOPS, SORRY!
HOW DO YOU FEEL, LITTLE MICROBE?
I THINK I'M OKAY. I DON'T HAVE A FEVER.
WOOF
MISSILE!
IF MISSILE AND I WERE CURED, THAT MEANT ALL OF OUR SCHOOLMATES WERE, TOO.
ERNEST HAD TRULY SAVED THE SCHOOL FROM THE ZOMBIE-VIRUS...
DADDY WAS ON HIS WAY TO SEE GRANDPA BUG AT THE HOSPITAL...
HE'D MADE A LITTLE DETOUR BY OUR HOUSE TO SEE US.
HE'S TAKING OFF AGAIN IN A FEW HOURS... JUST AFTER WE EAT.
HE TRIED TO REASSURE US, BUT I COULD SEE HE WAS WORRIED...

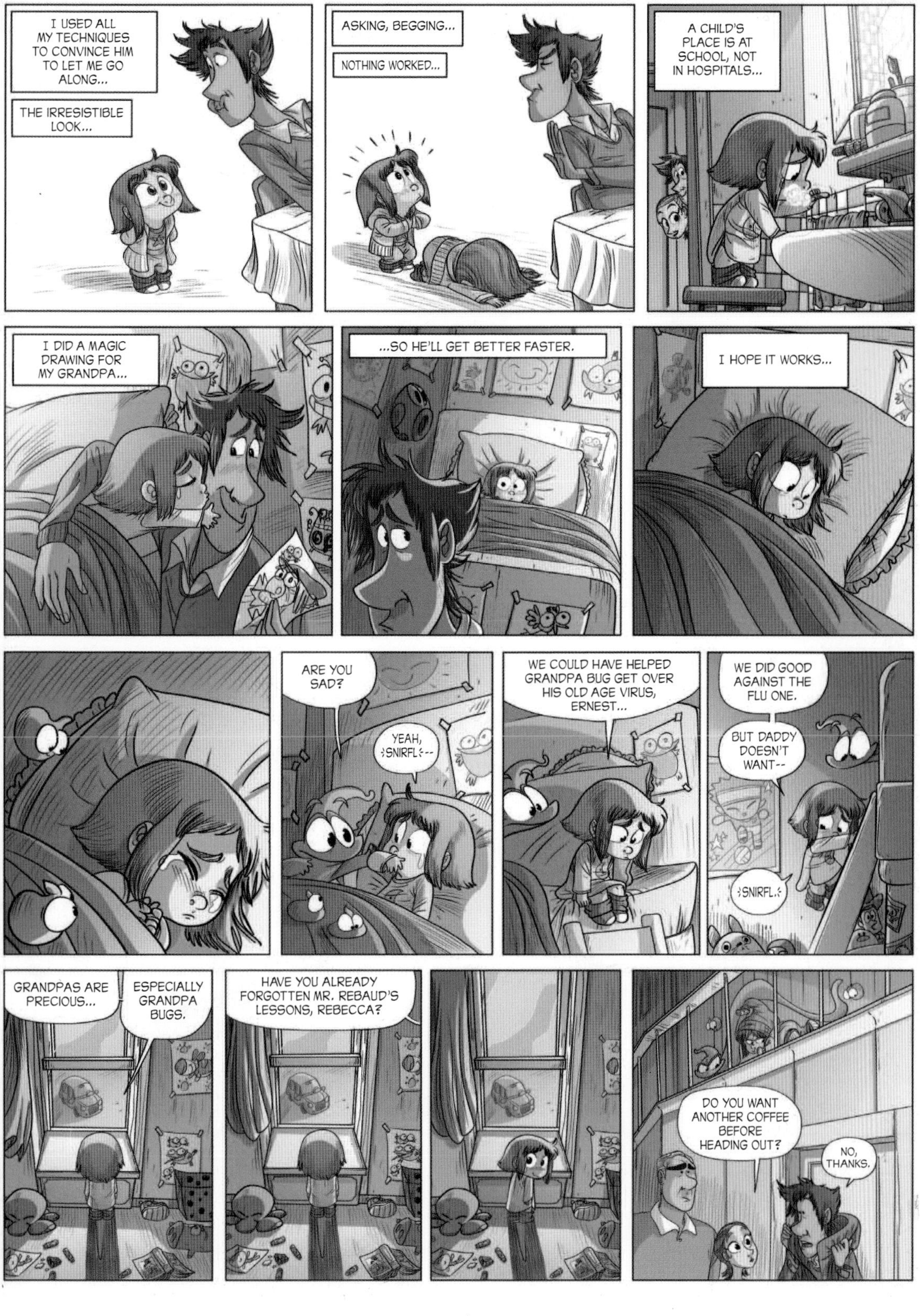
I USED ALL MY TECHNIQUES TO CONVINCE HIM TO LET ME GO ALONG...
THE IRRESISTIBLE LOOK...
ASKING, BEGGING...
NOTHING WORKED...
A CHILD'S PLACE IS AT SCHOOL, NOT IN HOSPITALS...
I DID A MAGIC DRAWING FOR MY GRANDPA...
...SO HE'LL GET BETTER FASTER.
I HOPE IT WORKS...
ARE YOU SAD?
YEAH, ⸗SNIRFL⸗--
WE COULD HAVE HELPED GRANDPA BUG GET OVER HIS OLD AGE VIRUS, ERNEST...
WE DID GOOD AGAINST THE FLU ONE.
BUT DADDY DOESN'T WANT--
⸗SNIRFL.⸗
GRANDPAS ARE PRECIOUS...
ESPECIALLY GRANDPA BUGS.
HAVE YOU ALREADY FORGOTTEN MR. REBAUD'S LESSONS, REBECCA?
DO YOU WANT ANOTHER COFFEE BEFORE HEADING OUT?
NO, THANKS.

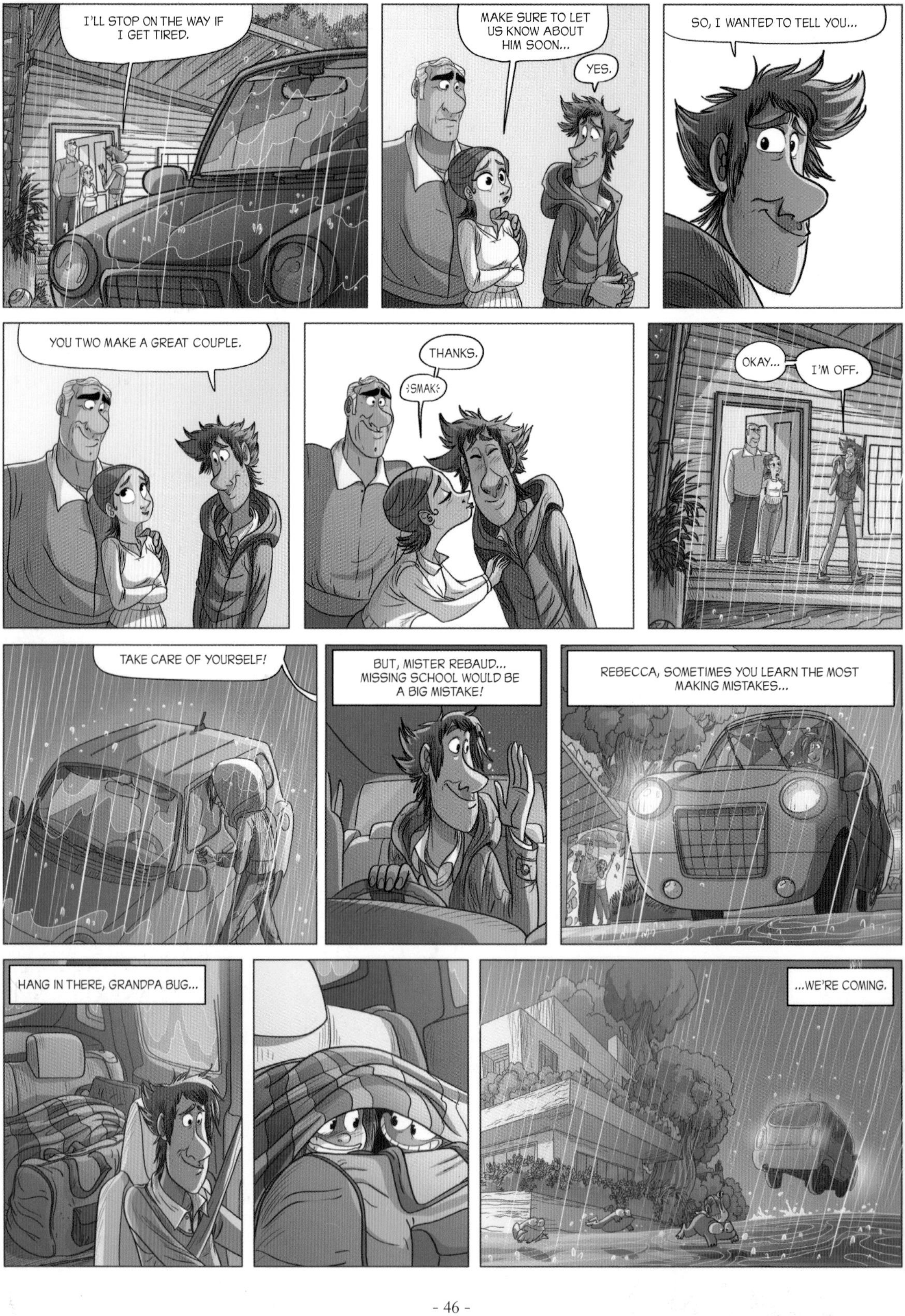
I'LL STOP ON THE WAY IF I GET TIRED.
MAKE SURE TO LET US KNOW ABOUT HIM SOON...
YES.
SO, I WANTED TO TELL YOU...
YOU TWO MAKE A GREAT COUPLE.
THANKS.
SMAK
OKAY...
I'M OFF.
TAKE CARE OF YOURSELF!
BUT, MISTER REBAUD... MISSING SCHOOL WOULD BE A BIG MISTAKE!
REBECCA, SOMETIMES YOU LEARN THE MOST MAKING MISTAKES...
HANG IN THERE, GRANDPA BUG...
...WE'RE COMING.

WATCH OUT FOR PAPERCUTZ

Hi, I'm Jim Salicrup, the Editor-in-Chief.
I'm finally fifty-six and a half!
Fifty-seven soon!

It's back-to-work
Something I look forward to everyday,
especially when there's a new REBECCA & ERNEST to edit!
REBECCA & ERNEST, not to mention Guillaume Bianco and Antonello Dalena, are so cool.
Papercutz is dedicated to publishing great graphic novels for all ages, and ERNEST & REBECCA is
one of the best!

While the flu zombie-virus is "just a story," it may not be all that far-fetched.
Viruses seem to be getting stronger all the time, so it makes sense to be as careful as possible.
You always need to be careful.
Remember what happened to the Smurfs when one of them got bit by the Bzzz fly?
Everyone got infected!
The blue smurfs turned purple and were soon biting other smurfs and turning them purple too! You can
get the whole story in THE SMURFS #1 from Papercutz.
Some people consider that story a virtual "zombie" story. In PAPERCUTZ SLICES #5 we did a
parody of a popular zombie comicbook series that was turned into a hit TV series, but I won't mention
the title here— Rebecca's mom might object. Maybe we should've done a series called THE LOVING
DEAD instead?
While we don't really have to worry about zombies, we can all take a little better care of ourselves.
It's really no fun getting sick, so the best thing is to avoid anything that could possibly make us sick.
While some of you may think that fifty-seven is old, I'm still not quite as old as Grandpa Bug. Speaking
of whom, I hope he's okay. I've grown very attached to him, as well as Rebecca, Ernest, Coralie, and
all the others in this awesome graphic novel series, and I've got my fingers crossed that everything
will turn out okay. Seriously, I cry enough over stuff that happens in ERNEST & REBECCA, I don't
think I can handle anything seriously bad happening to Grandpa Bug. Let's hope the title of the next
volume is not falsely optimistic. So, enjoy this volume of ERNEST & REBECCA, and we'll meet again
in ERNEST & REBECCA #6 "The Box of Jokes."

Thanks,

JIM

STAY IN TOUCH!

EMAIL: salicrup@papercutz.com
WEB: papercutz.com
TWITTER: @papercutzgn
FACEBOOK: PAPERCUTZGRAPHICNOVELS
FAN MAIL: Papercutz, 160 Broadway, Suite 700, East Wing,
                New York, NY 10038

See
Ernest and Rebecca again
in volume 6, titled:
"The Box of Jokes."

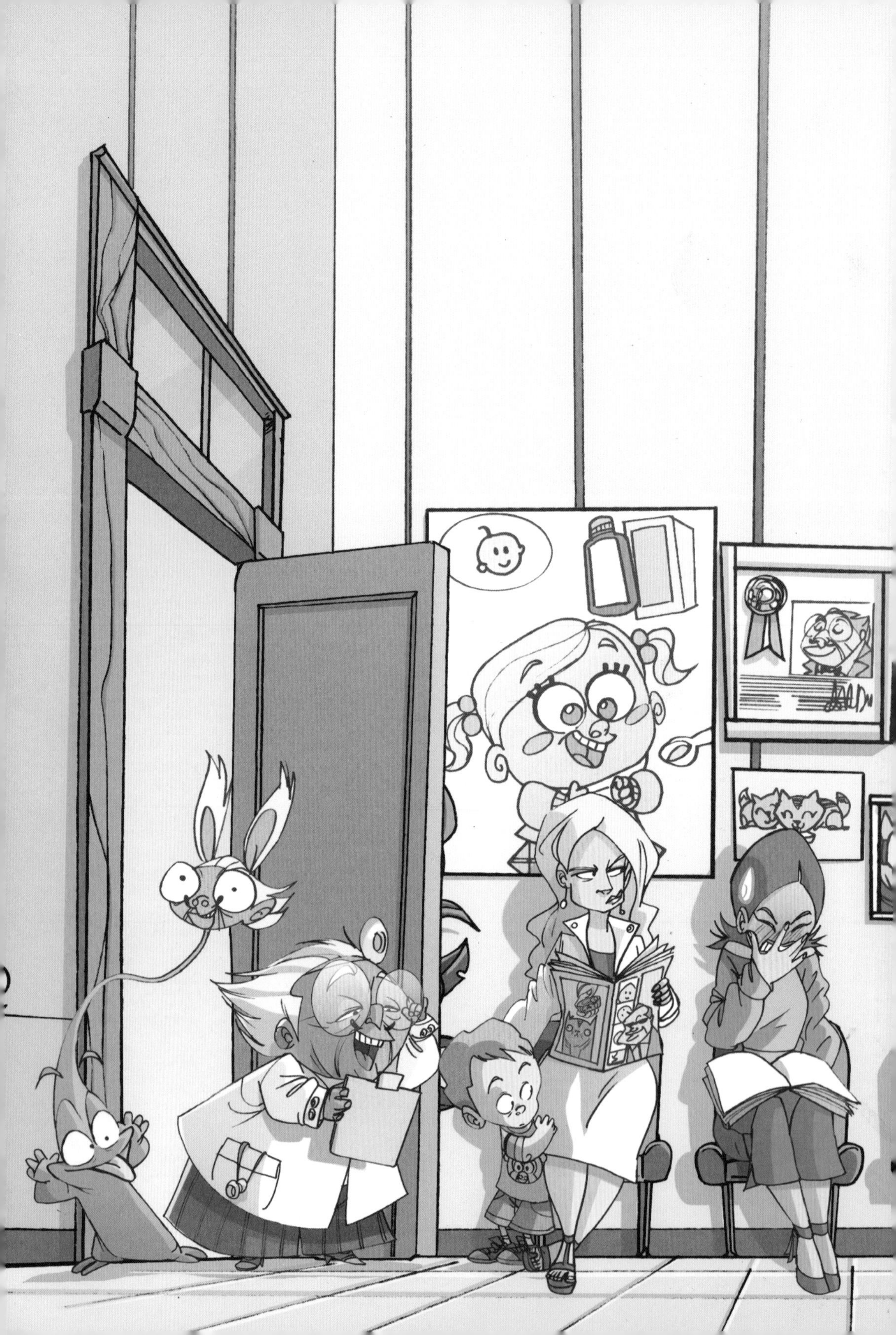